BATMAN TEENAGE MUTANT NINJA TURTLES ADVENTURES

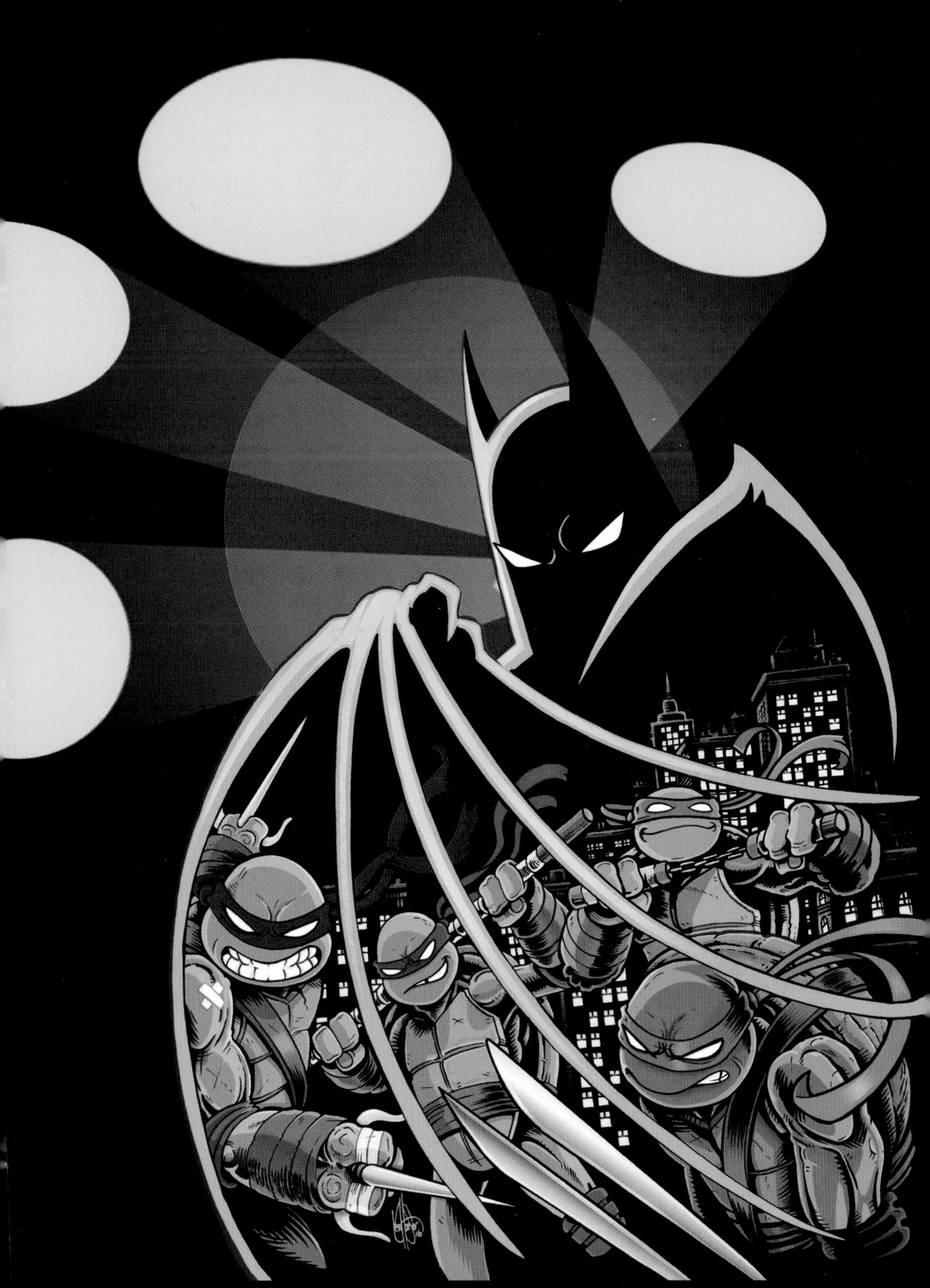

Batman / Teenage Mutant Ninja Turtles Adventures
is published by Stone Arch Books,
A Capstone Imprint
1710 Roe Crest Drive
North Mankato, Minnesota 56003
www.mycapstonepub.com

Originally published as BATMAN/TEENAGE MUTANT NINJA
TURTLES ADVENTURES issue #5.

Cataloging-in-Publication Data is available at the
Library of Congress website:
ISBN 978-1-4965-7386-5 (library binding)
ISBN 978-1-4965-7393-3 (eBook PDF)

Summary: Watch out, New York City! Mad Hatter
is up to something evil. Batman and the Teenage
Mutant Ninja Turtles join forces to put a stop to his
crazy plans.

STONE ARCH BOOKS
Donald Lemke Editorial Director
Gena Chester Editor
Hilary Wacholz Art Director
Kathy McColley Production Specialist

Batman created by Bob Kane with Bill Finger

BATMAN TEENAGE MUTANT NINJA TURTLES ADVENTURES

THROUGH THE LOOKING GLASS

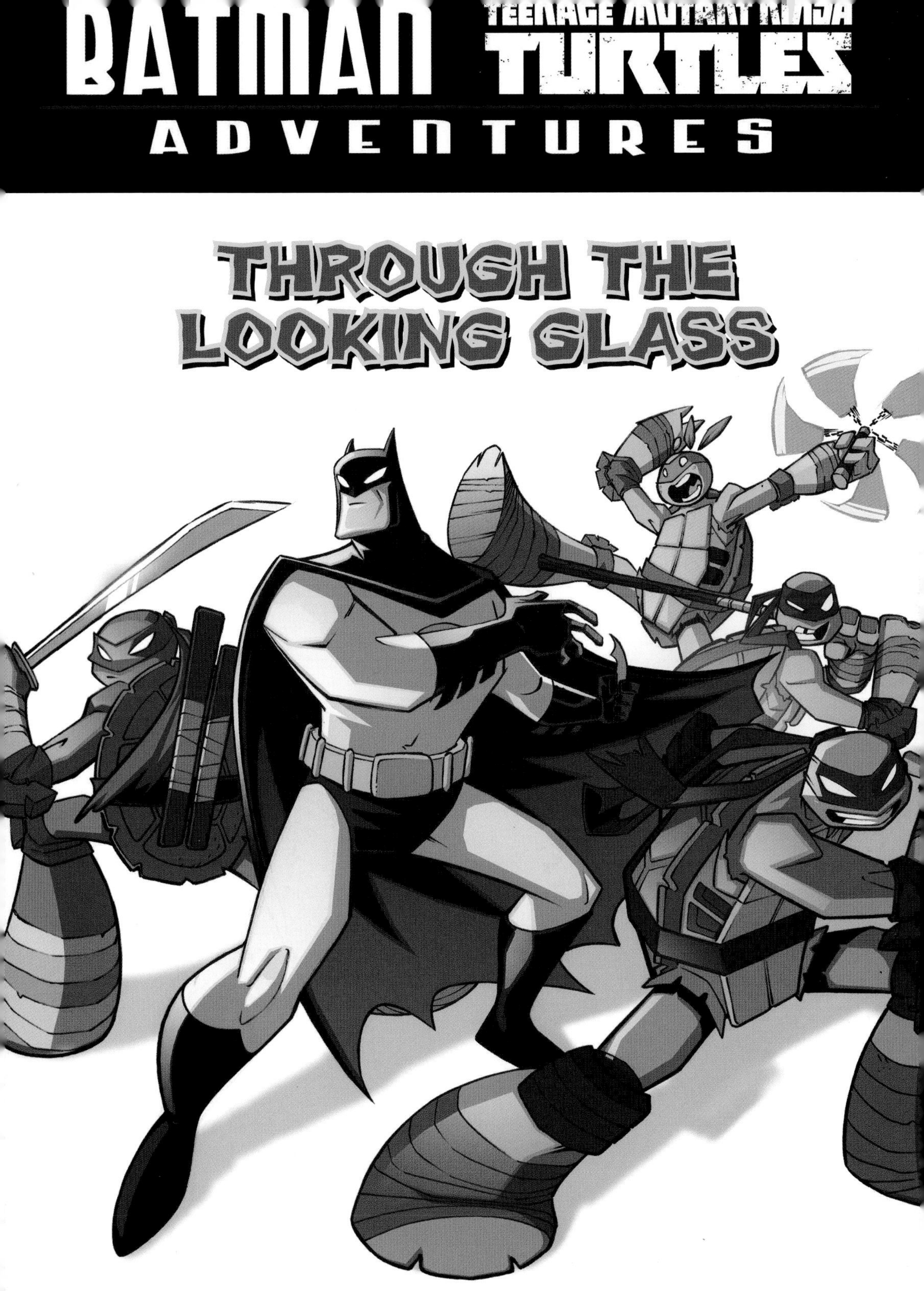

WRITER: MATTHEW K. MANNING | ARTIST: JON SOMMARIVA
INKER: SEAN PARSONS | COLORIST: LEONARDO ITO

STONE ARCH BOOKS
a capstone imprint

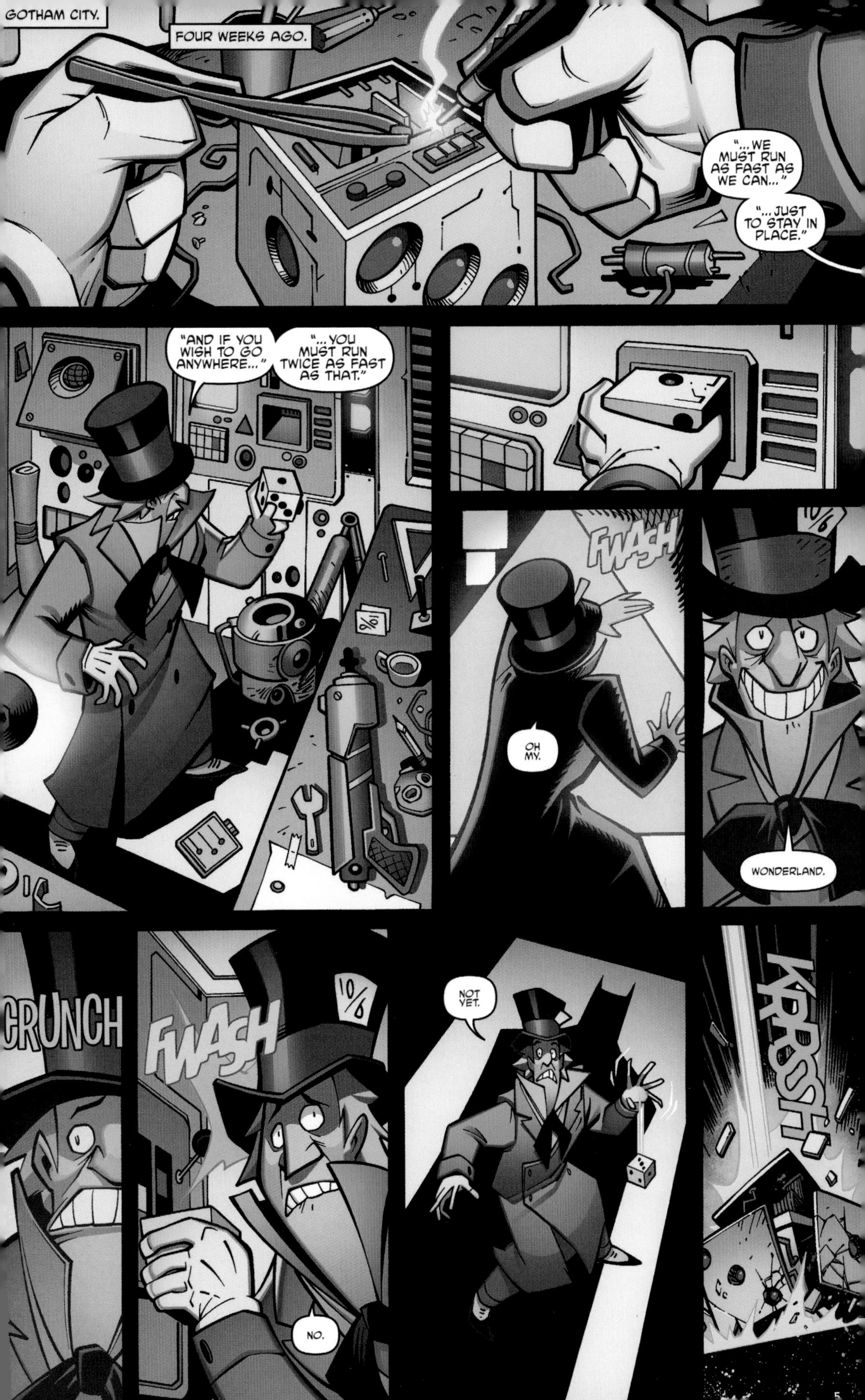
GOTHAM CITY.
FOUR WEEKS AGO.
"...WE MUST RUN AS FAST AS WE CAN..."
"...JUST TO STAY IN PLACE."
"AND IF YOU WISH TO GO ANYWHERE..."
"...YOU MUST RUN TWICE AS FAST AS THAT."
FWASH
OH MY.
WONDERLAND.
CRUNCH
FWASH
NO.
NOT YET.

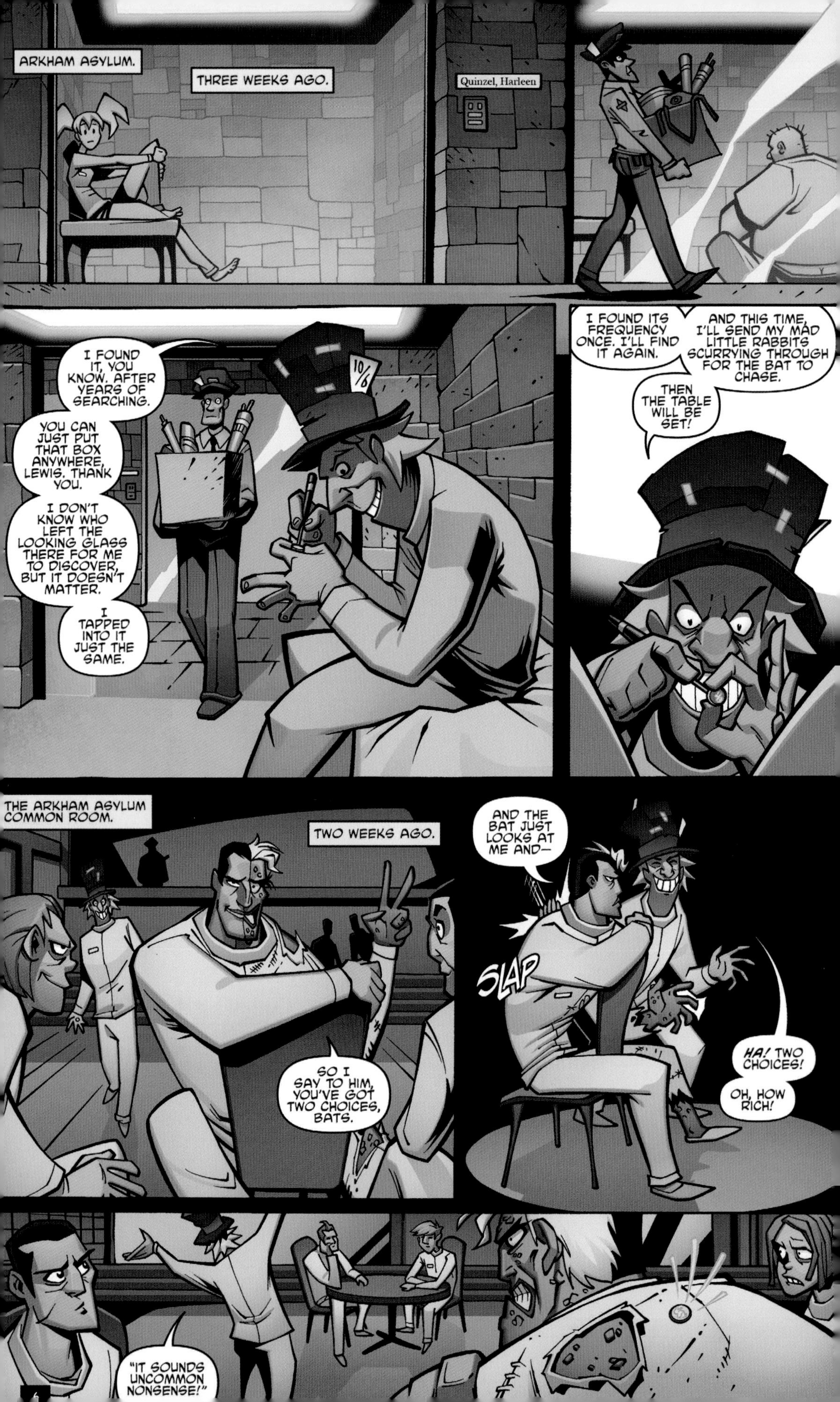
ARKHAM ASYLUM.
THREE WEEKS AGO.
Quinzel, Harleen
I FOUND IT, YOU KNOW. AFTER YEARS OF SEARCHING.
YOU CAN JUST PUT THAT BOX ANYWHERE, LEWIS. THANK YOU.
I DON'T KNOW WHO LEFT THE LOOKING GLASS THERE FOR ME TO DISCOVER, BUT IT DOESN'T MATTER.
I TAPPED INTO IT JUST THE SAME.
10/6
I FOUND ITS FREQUENCY ONCE. I'LL FIND IT AGAIN.
AND THIS TIME, I'LL SEND MY MAD LITTLE RABBITS SCURRYING THROUGH FOR THE BAT TO CHASE.
THEN THE TABLE WILL BE SET!
THE ARKHAM ASYLUM COMMON ROOM.
TWO WEEKS AGO.
SO I SAY TO HIM, YOU'VE GOT TWO CHOICES, BATS.
AND THE BAT JUST LOOKS AT ME AND—
SLAP
HA! TWO CHOICES!
OH, HOW RICH!
"IT SOUNDS UNCOMMON NONSENSE!"

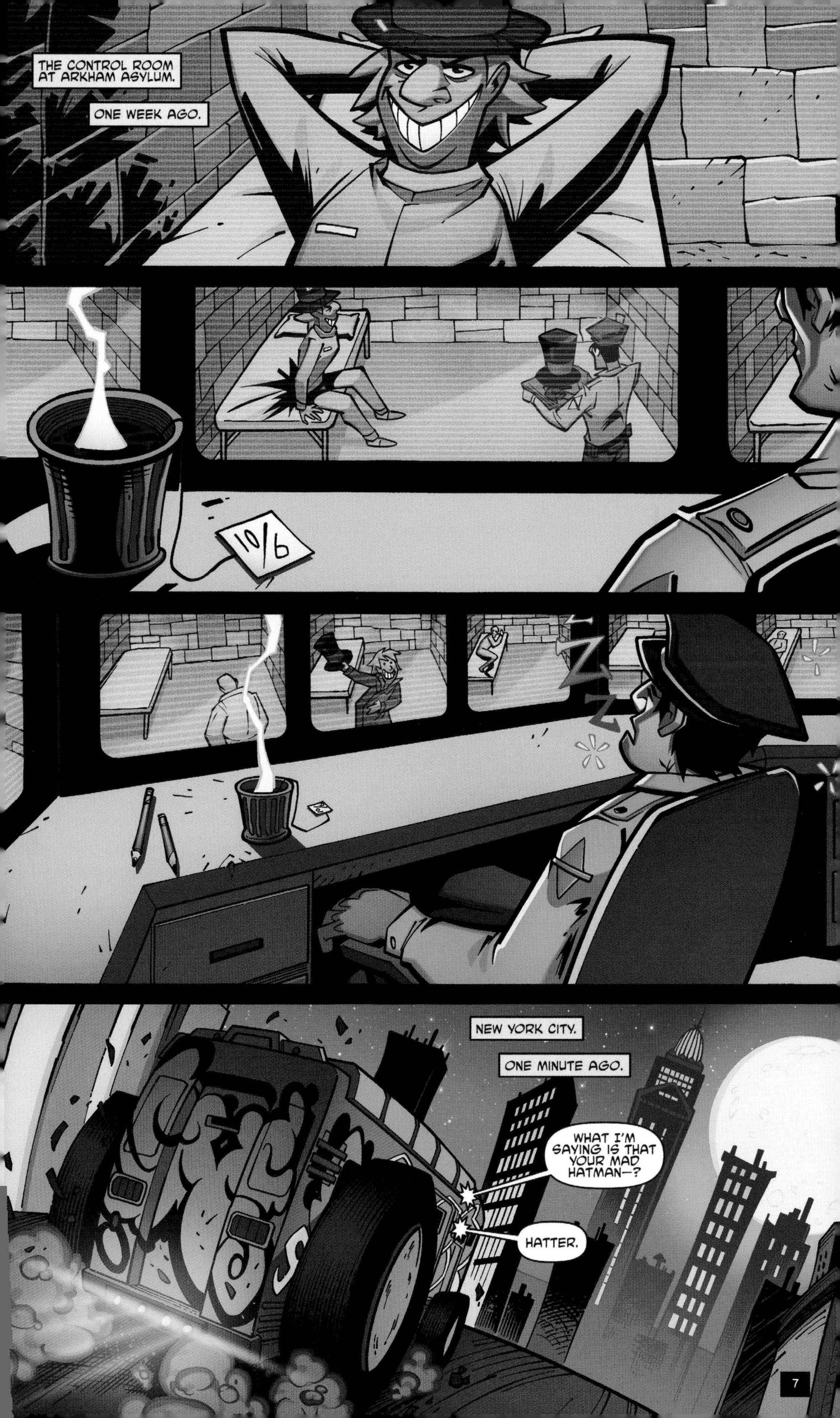
THE CONTROL ROOM AT ARKHAM ASYLUM.
ONE WEEK AGO.
10/6
NEW YORK CITY.
ONE MINUTE AGO.
WHAT I'M SAYING IS THAT YOUR MAD HATMAN—?
HATTER.

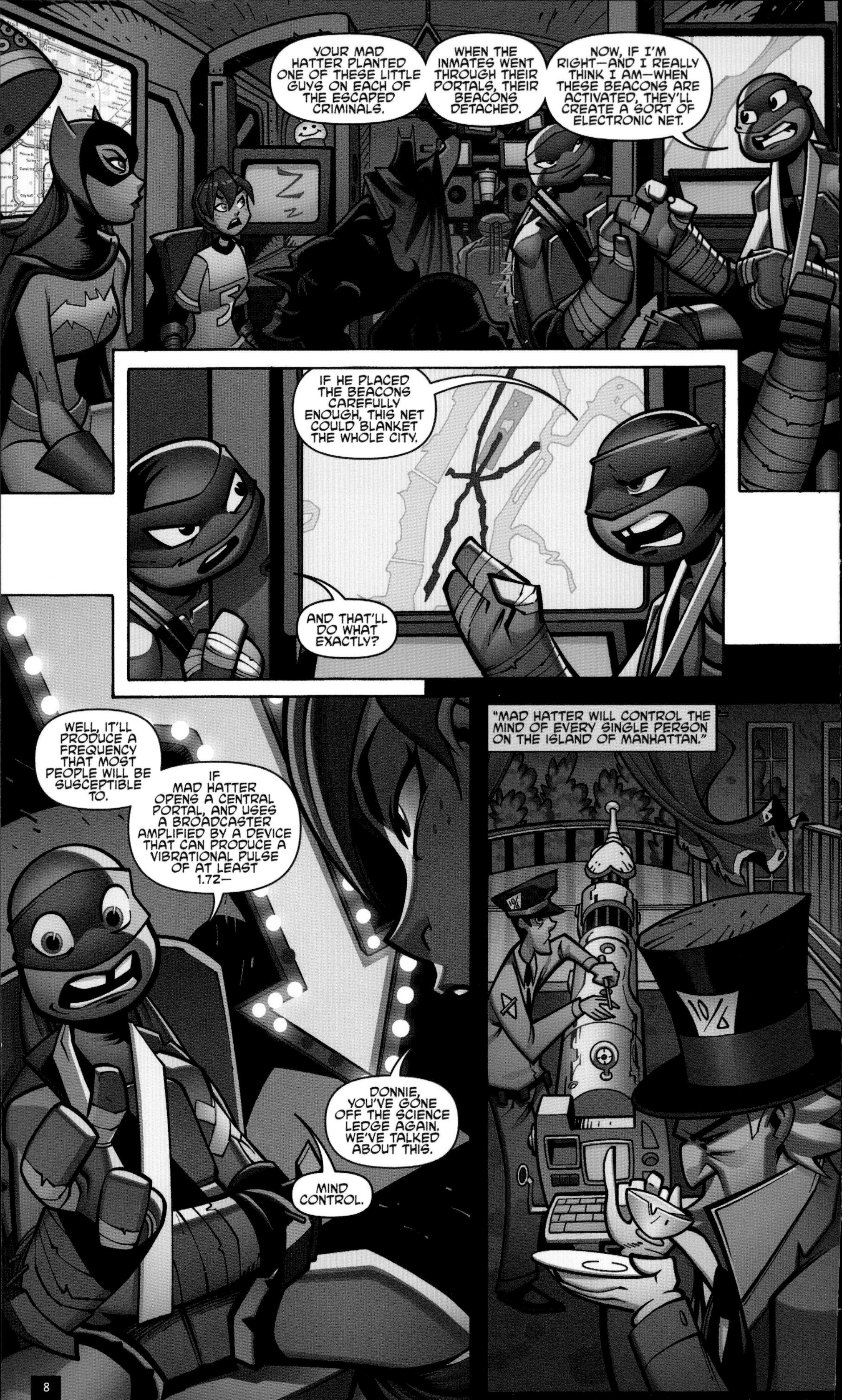

YOUR MAD HATTER PLANTED ONE OF THESE LITTLE GUYS ON EACH OF THE ESCAPED CRIMINALS.
WHEN THE INMATES WENT THROUGH THEIR PORTALS, THEIR BEACONS DETACHED.
NOW, IF I'M RIGHT—AND I REALLY THINK I AM—WHEN THESE BEACONS ARE ACTIVATED, THEY'LL CREATE A SORT OF ELECTRONIC NET.
IF HE PLACED THE BEACONS CAREFULLY ENOUGH, THIS NET COULD BLANKET THE WHOLE CITY.
AND THAT'LL DO WHAT EXACTLY?
WELL, IT'LL PRODUCE A FREQUENCY THAT MOST PEOPLE WILL BE SUSCEPTIBLE TO.
IF MAD HATTER OPENS A CENTRAL PORTAL, AND USES A BROADCASTER AMPLIFIED BY A DEVICE THAT CAN PRODUCE A VIBRATIONAL PULSE OF AT LEAST 1.72—
DONNIE, YOU'VE GONE OFF THE SCIENCE LEDGE AGAIN. WE'VE TALKED ABOUT THIS.
MIND CONTROL.
"MAD HATTER WILL CONTROL THE MIND OF EVERY SINGLE PERSON ON THE ISLAND OF MANHATTAN."
10/6

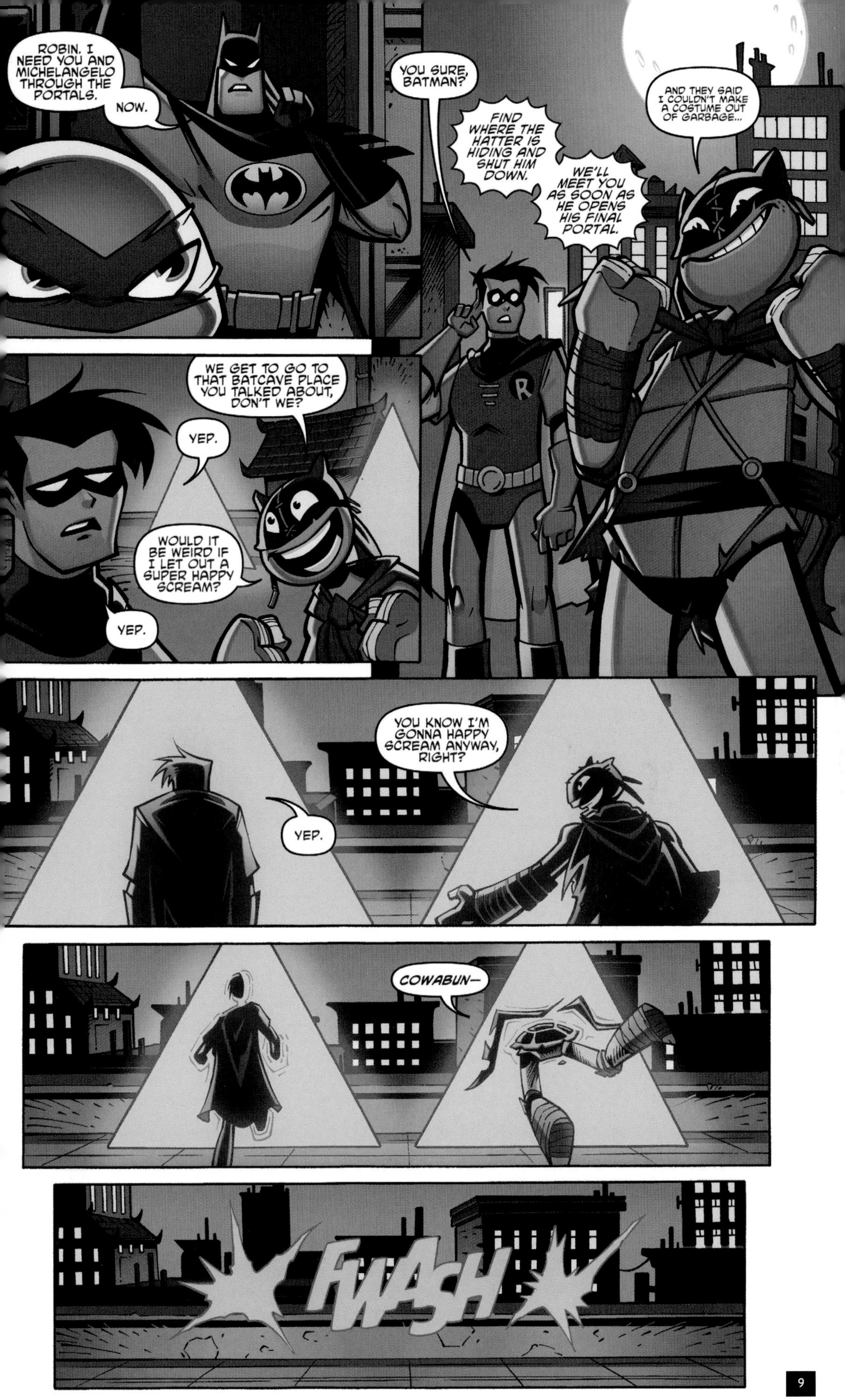
ROBIN. I NEED YOU AND MICHELANGELO THROUGH THE PORTALS.
NOW.
YOU SURE, BATMAN?
FIND WHERE THE HATTER IS HIDING AND SHUT HIM DOWN.
WE'LL MEET YOU AS SOON AS HE OPENS HIS FINAL PORTAL.
AND THEY SAID I COULDN'T MAKE A COSTUME OUT OF GARBAGE...
WE GET TO GO TO THAT BATCAVE PLACE YOU TALKED ABOUT, DON'T WE?
YEP.
WOULD IT BE WEIRD IF I LET OUT A SUPER HAPPY SCREAM?
YEP.
YOU KNOW I'M GONNA HAPPY SCREAM ANYWAY, RIGHT?
YEP.
COWABUN—
FWASH

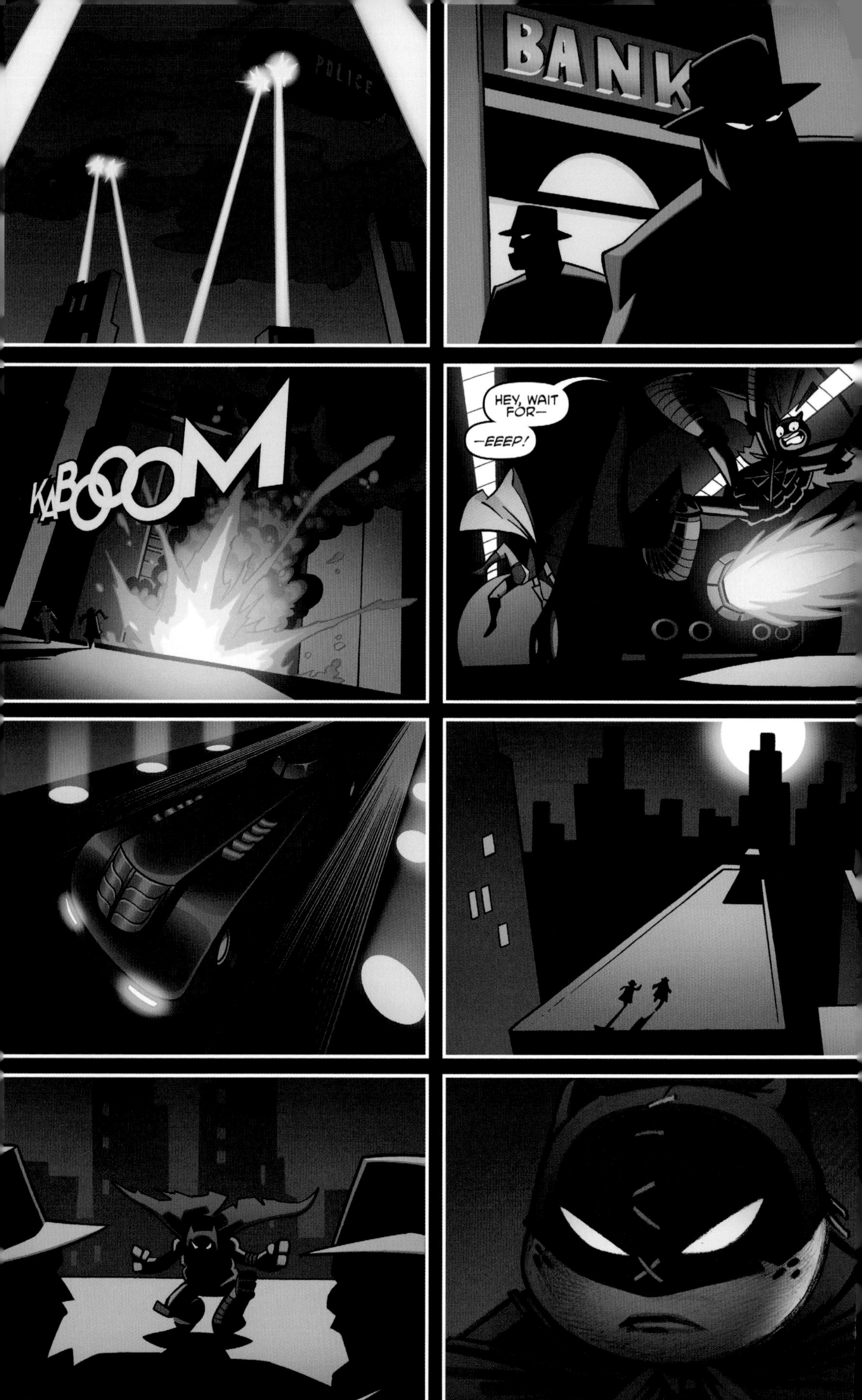
POLICE
BANK
KABOOOM
HEY, WAIT FOR—
—EEEP!

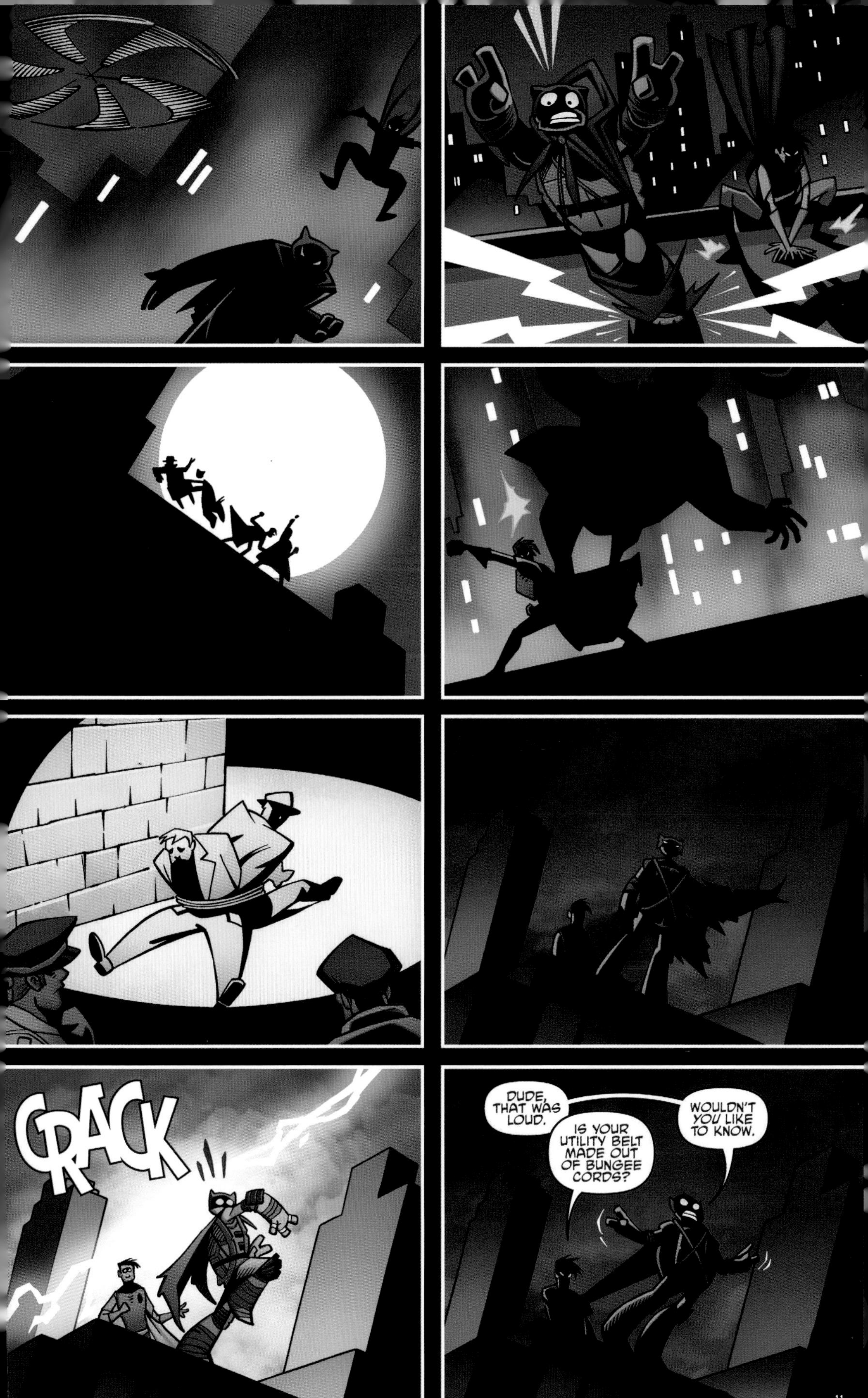
CRACK
DUDE, THAT WAS LOUD.
IS YOUR UTILITY BELT MADE OUT OF BUNGEE CORDS?
WOULDN'T YOU LIKE TO KNOW.

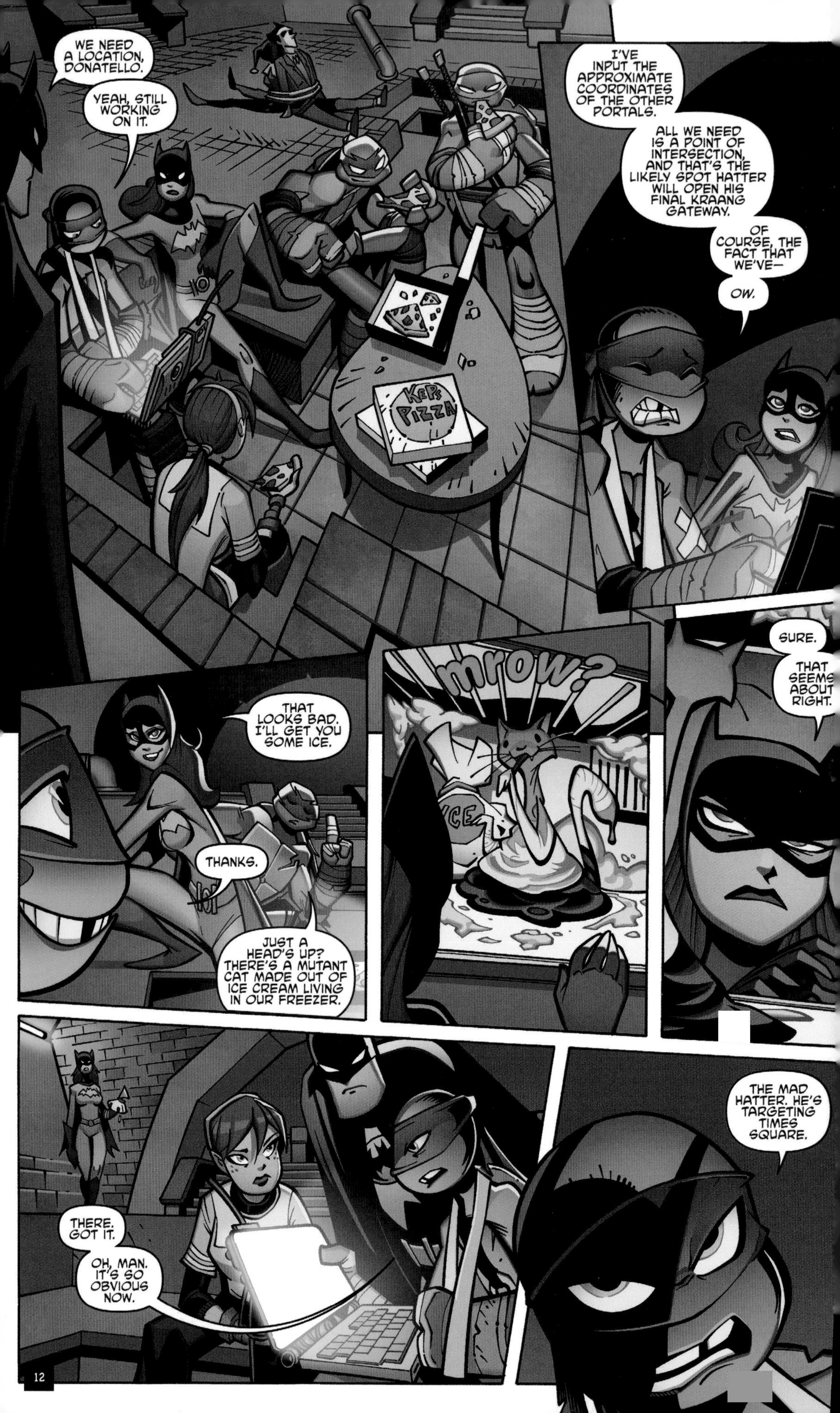

WE NEED A LOCATION, DONATELLO.
YEAH, STILL WORKING ON IT.
KEP'S PIZZA
I'VE INPUT THE APPROXIMATE COORDINATES OF THE OTHER PORTALS.
ALL WE NEED IS A POINT OF INTERSECTION, AND THAT'S THE LIKELY SPOT HATTER WILL OPEN HIS FINAL KRAANG GATEWAY.
OF COURSE, THE FACT THAT WE'VE—
OW.
THAT LOOKS BAD. I'LL GET YOU SOME ICE.
THANKS.
JUST A HEAD'S UP? THERE'S A MUTANT CAT MADE OUT OF ICE CREAM LIVING IN OUR FREEZER.
mrow?
SURE.
THAT SEEMS ABOUT RIGHT.
THERE. GOT IT.
OH, MAN. IT'S SO OBVIOUS NOW.
THE MAD HATTER. HE'S TARGETING TIMES SQUARE.

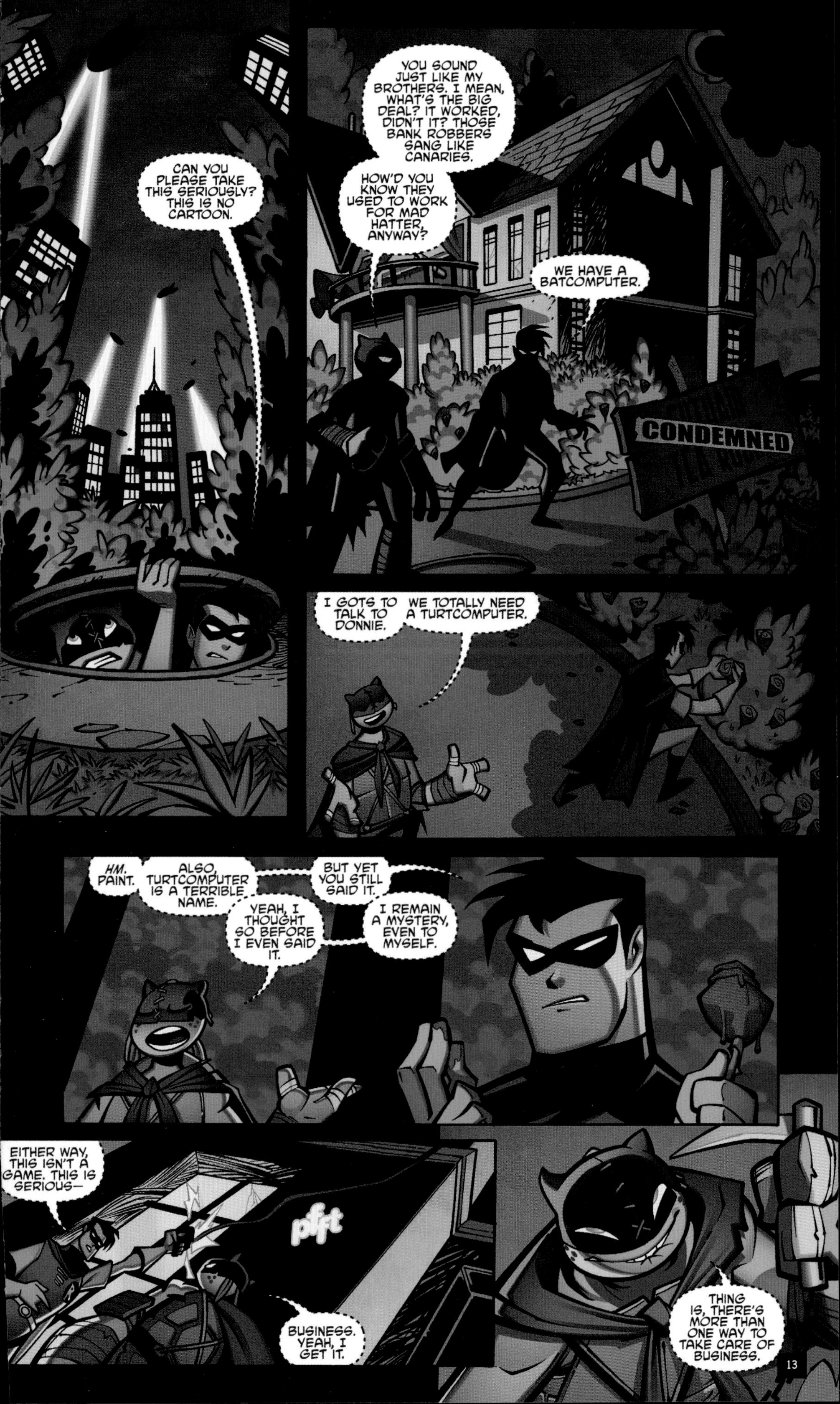
CAN YOU PLEASE TAKE THIS SERIOUSLY? THIS IS NO CARTOON.
YOU SOUND JUST LIKE MY BROTHERS. I MEAN, WHAT'S THE BIG DEAL? IT WORKED, DIDN'T IT? THOSE BANK ROBBERS SANG LIKE CANARIES.
HOW'D YOU KNOW THEY USED TO WORK FOR MAD HATTER, ANYWAY?
WE HAVE A BATCOMPUTER.
CONDEMNED
I GOTS TO TALK TO DONNIE.
WE TOTALLY NEED A TURTCOMPUTER.
HM. PAINT.
ALSO, TURTCOMPUTER IS A TERRIBLE NAME.
YEAH, I THOUGHT SO BEFORE I EVEN SAID IT.
BUT YET YOU STILL SAID IT.
I REMAIN A MYSTERY, EVEN TO MYSELF.
EITHER WAY, THIS ISN'T A GAME. THIS IS SERIOUS—
pfft
BUSINESS. YEAH, I GET IT.
THING IS, THERE'S MORE THAN ONE WAY TO TAKE CARE OF BUSINESS.

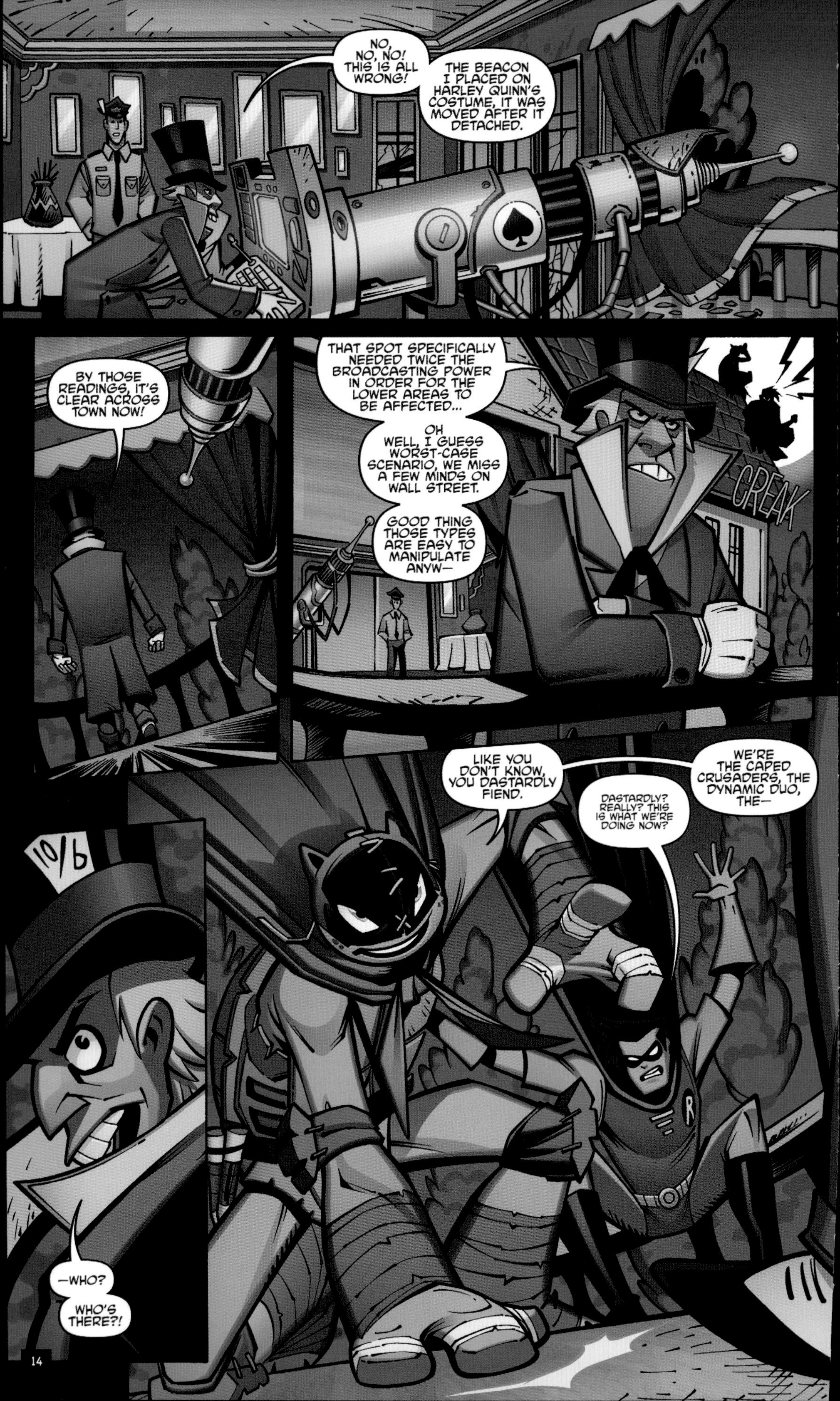
NO, NO, NO! THIS IS ALL WRONG!
THE BEACON I PLACED ON HARLEY QUINN'S COSTUME, IT WAS MOVED AFTER IT DETACHED.
BY THOSE READINGS, IT'S CLEAR ACROSS TOWN NOW!
THAT SPOT SPECIFICALLY NEEDED TWICE THE BROADCASTING POWER IN ORDER FOR THE LOWER AREAS TO BE AFFECTED...
OH WELL, I GUESS WORST-CASE SCENARIO, WE MISS A FEW MINDS ON WALL STREET.
GOOD THING THOSE TYPES ARE EASY TO MANIPULATE ANYW—
CREAK
LIKE YOU DON'T KNOW, YOU DASTARDLY FIEND.
WE'RE THE CAPED CRUSADERS, THE DYNAMIC DUO, THE—
DASTARDLY? REALLY? THIS IS WHAT WE'RE DOING NOW?
10/6
—WHO?
WHO'S THERE?!

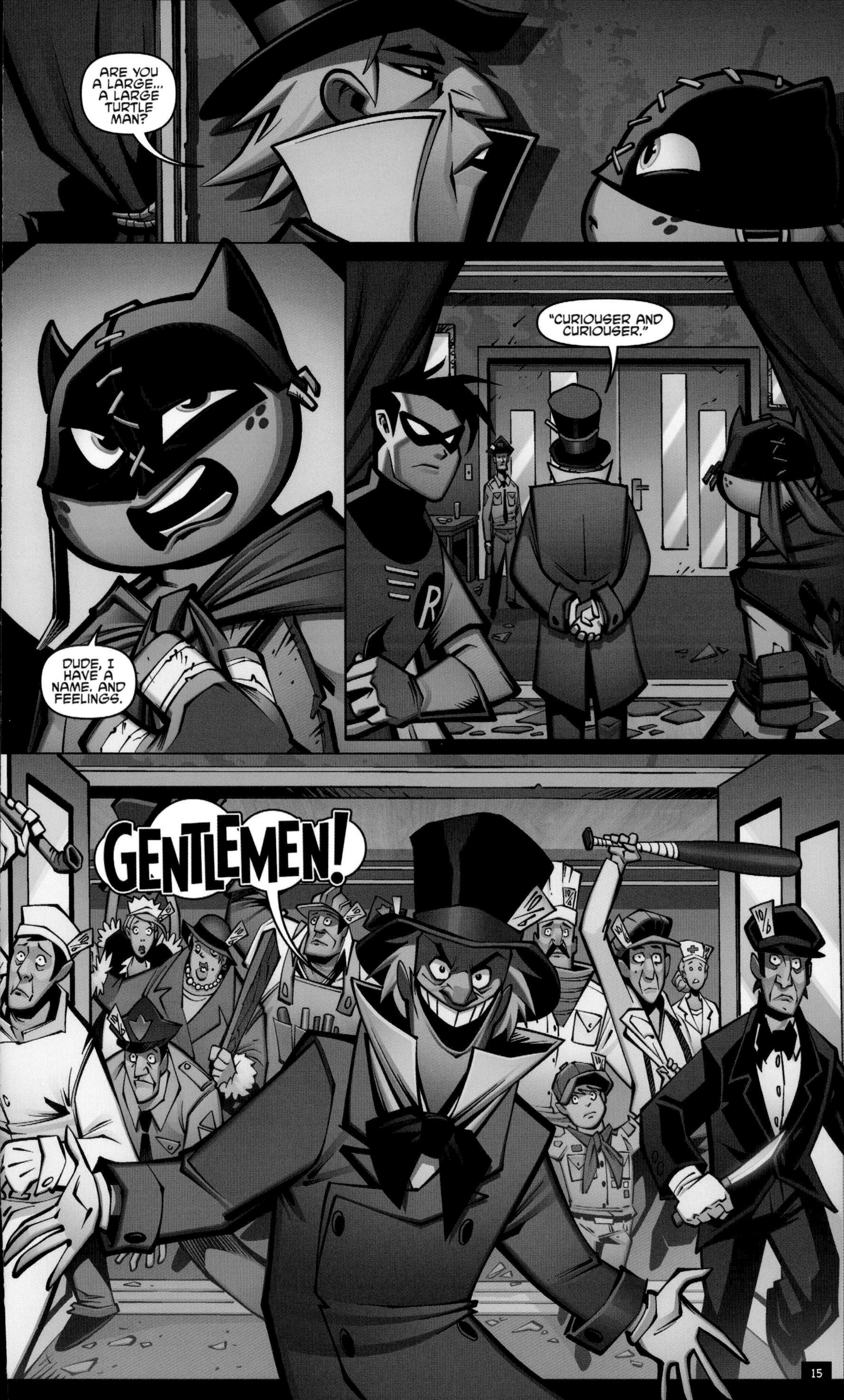
ARE YOU A LARGE... A LARGE TURTLE MAN?
DUDE, I HAVE A NAME. AND FEELINGS.
"CURIOUSER AND CURIOUSER."
GENTLEMEN!

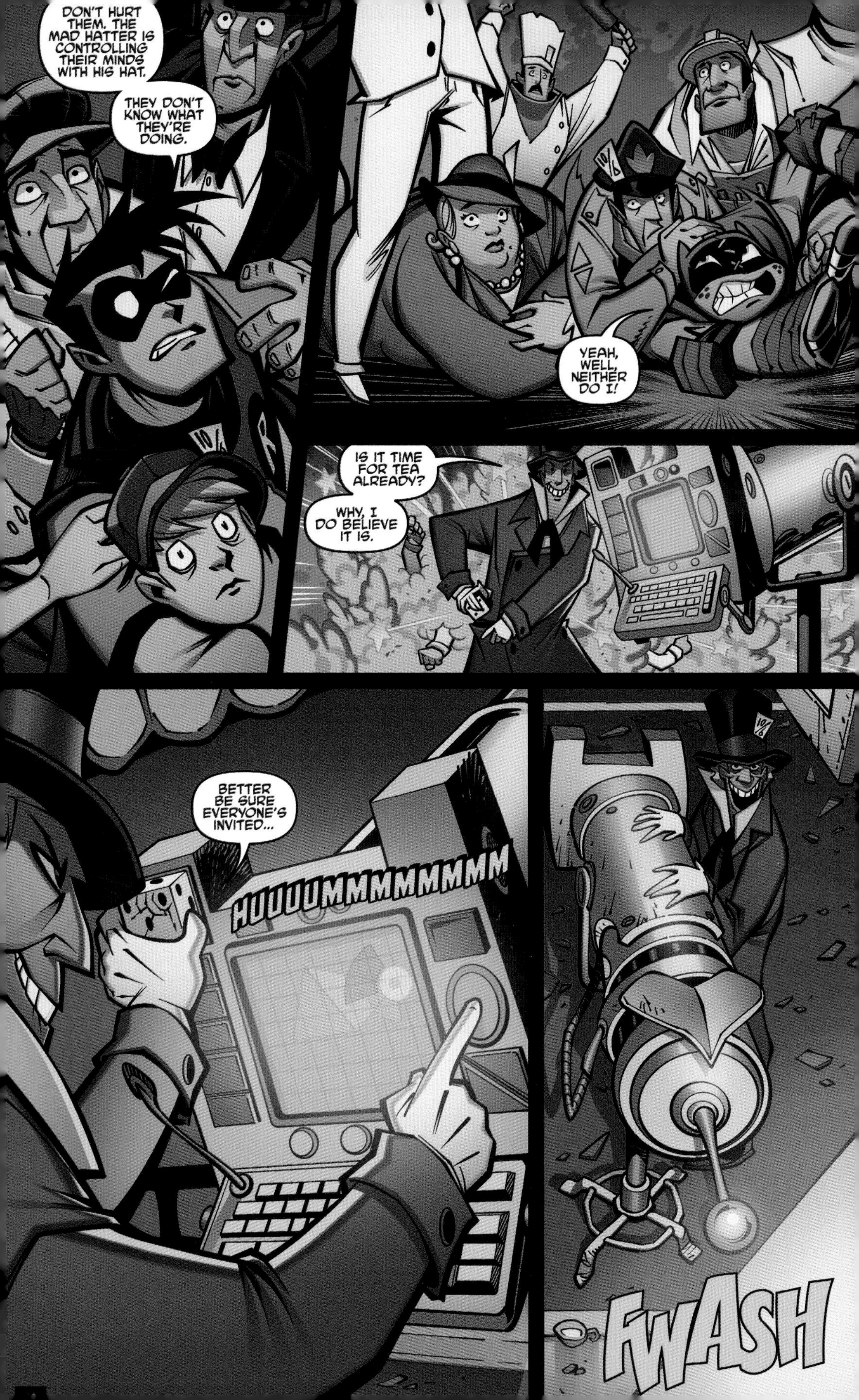
DON'T HURT THEM. THE MAD HATTER IS CONTROLLING THEIR MINDS WITH HIS HAT.
THEY DON'T KNOW WHAT THEY'RE DOING.
YEAH, WELL, NEITHER DO I!
IS IT TIME FOR TEA ALREADY?
WHY, I DO BELIEVE IT IS.
BETTER BE SURE EVERYONE'S INVITED...
HUUUUMMMMMMMMMM
FWASH

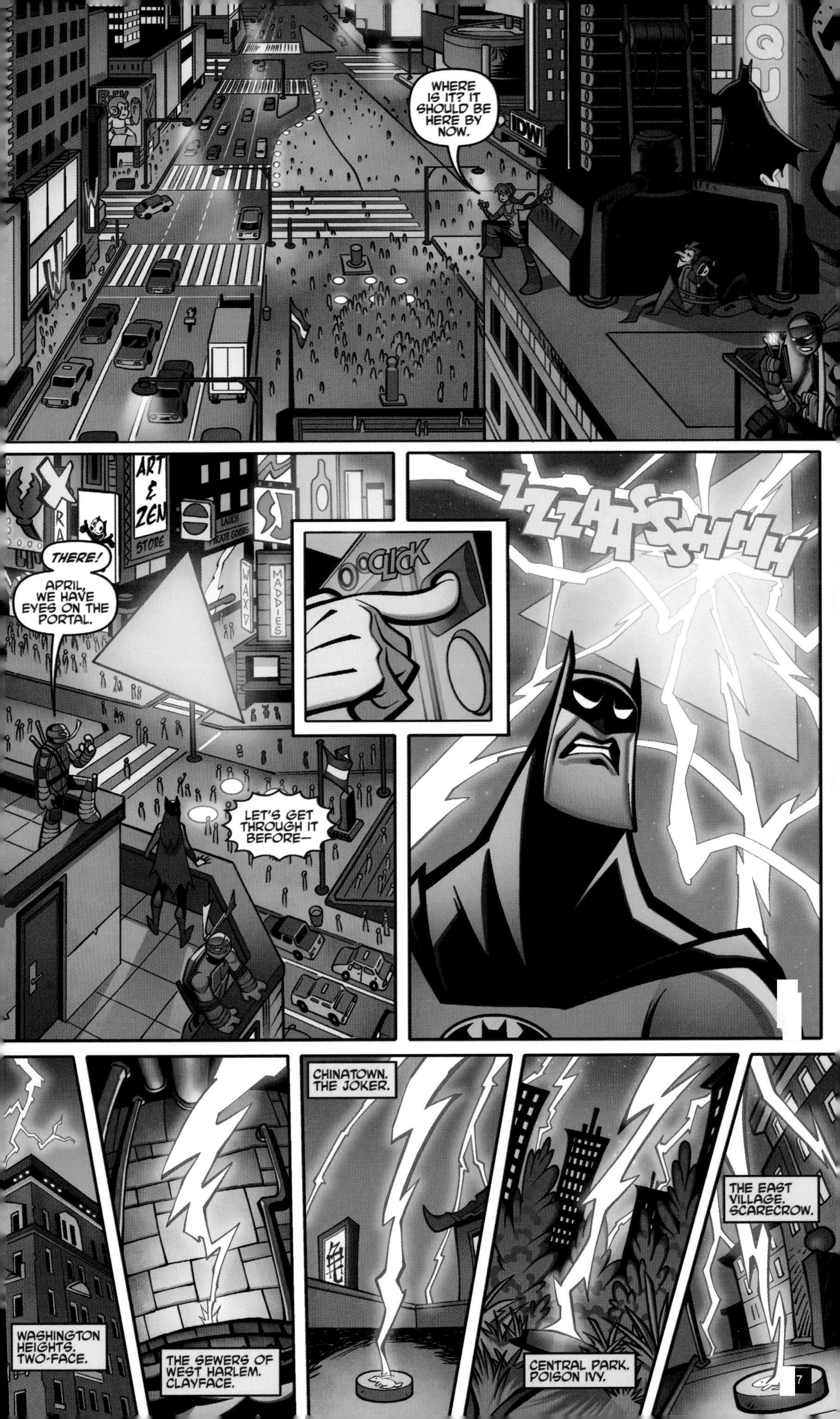

WHERE IS IT? IT SHOULD BE HERE BY NOW.
IDW
ART & ZEN STORE
WAX
MADDIES
THERE!
APRIL, WE HAVE EYES ON THE PORTAL.
LET'S GET THROUGH IT BEFORE—
CLICK
ZZZAASHHH
WASHINGTON HEIGHTS. TWO-FACE.
THE SEWERS OF WEST HARLEM. CLAYFACE.
CHINATOWN. THE JOKER.
CENTRAL PARK. POISON IVY.
THE EAST VILLAGE. SCARECROW.

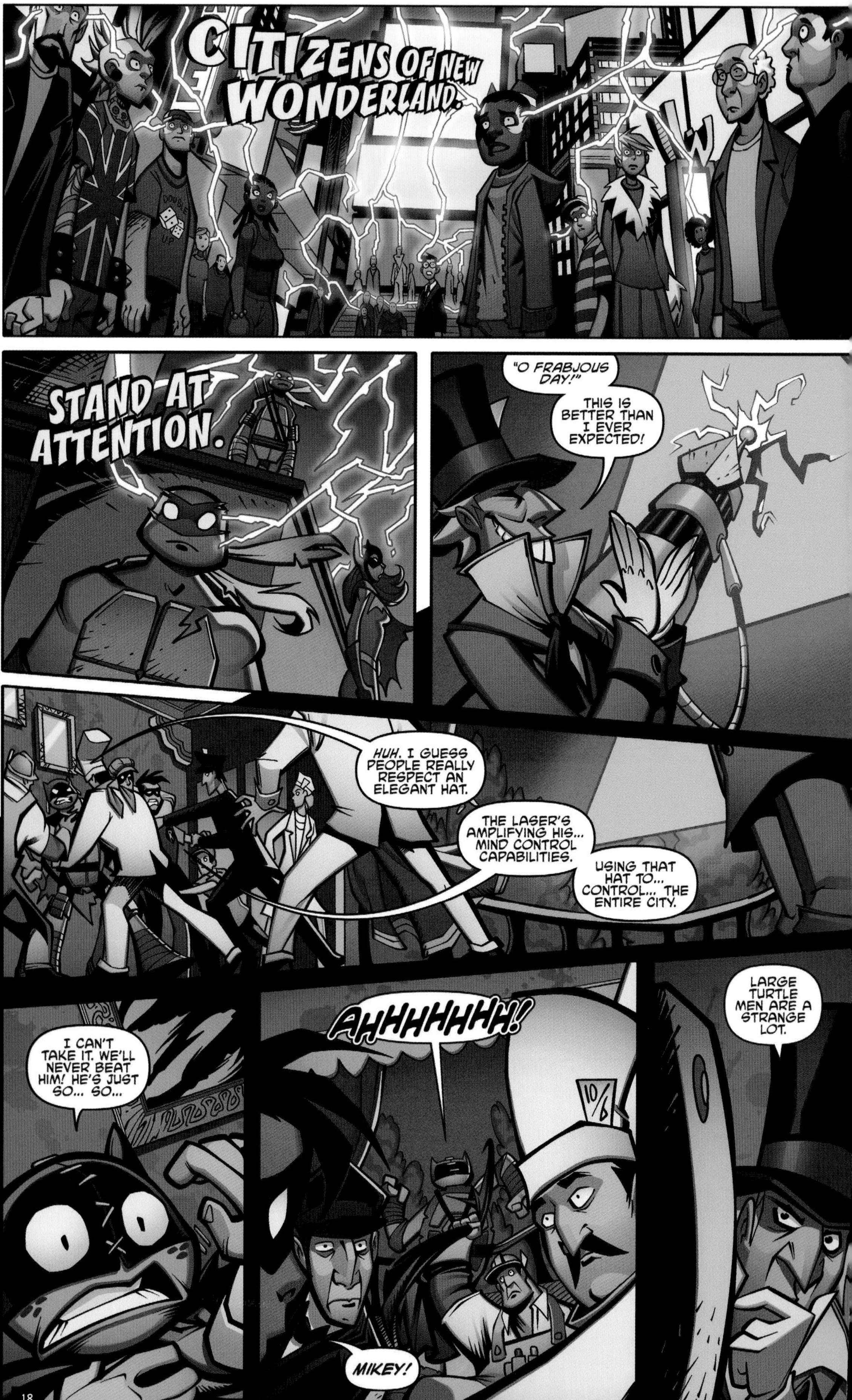
CITIZENS OF NEW WONDERLAND.
STAND AT ATTENTION.
"O FRABJOUS DAY!"
THIS IS BETTER THAN I EVER EXPECTED!
HUH. I GUESS PEOPLE REALLY RESPECT AN ELEGANT HAT.
THE LASER'S AMPLIFYING HIS... MIND CONTROL CAPABILITIES.
USING THAT HAT TO... CONTROL... THE ENTIRE CITY.
I CAN'T TAKE IT. WE'LL NEVER BEAT HIM! HE'S JUST SO... SO...
AHHHHHHH!
10/6
MIKEY!
LARGE TURTLE MEN ARE A STRANGE LOT.

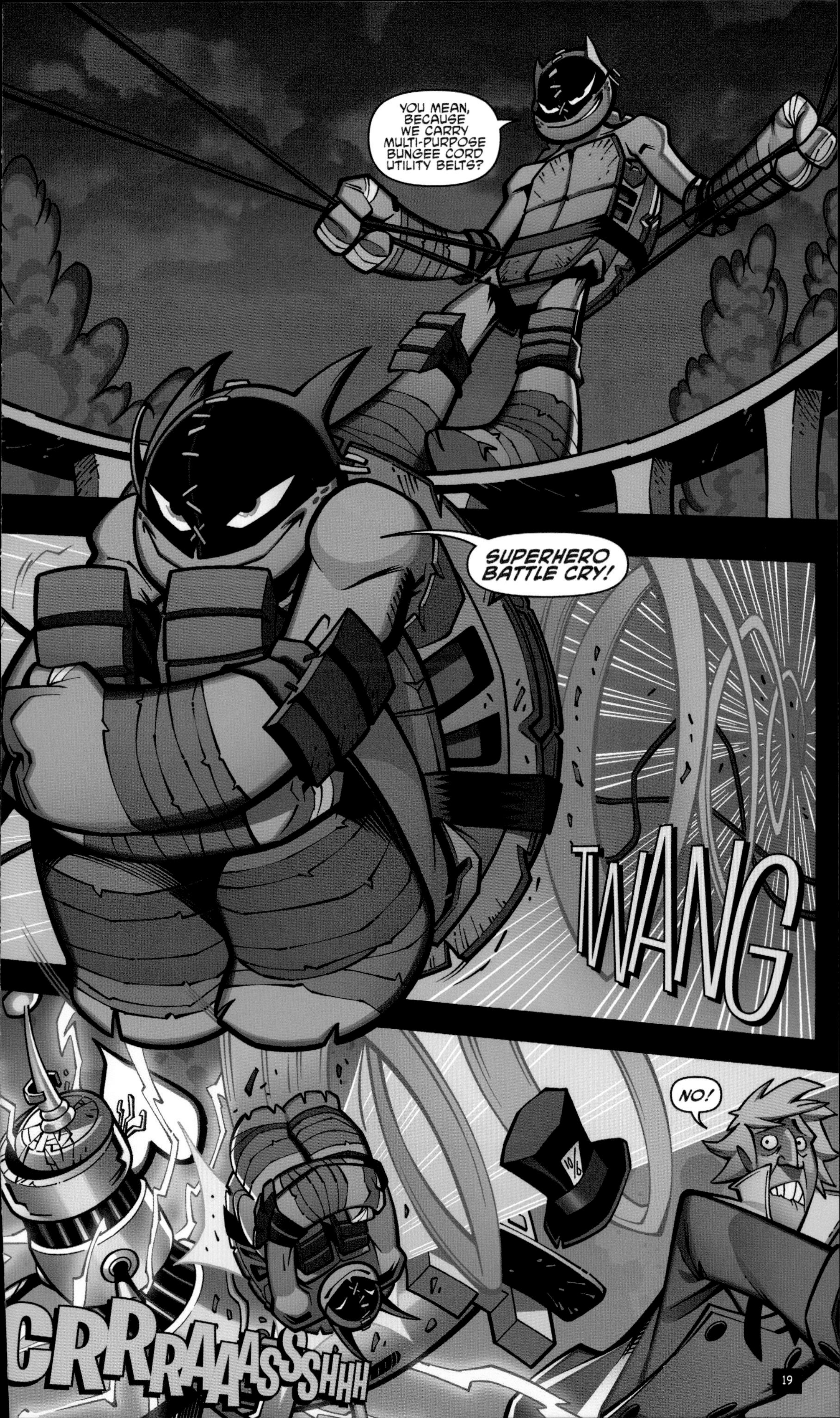

YOU MEAN, BECAUSE WE CARRY MULTI-PURPOSE BUNGEE CORD UTILITY BELTS?
SUPERHERO BATTLE CRY!
TWANG
NO!
CRRRAAASSSHHH

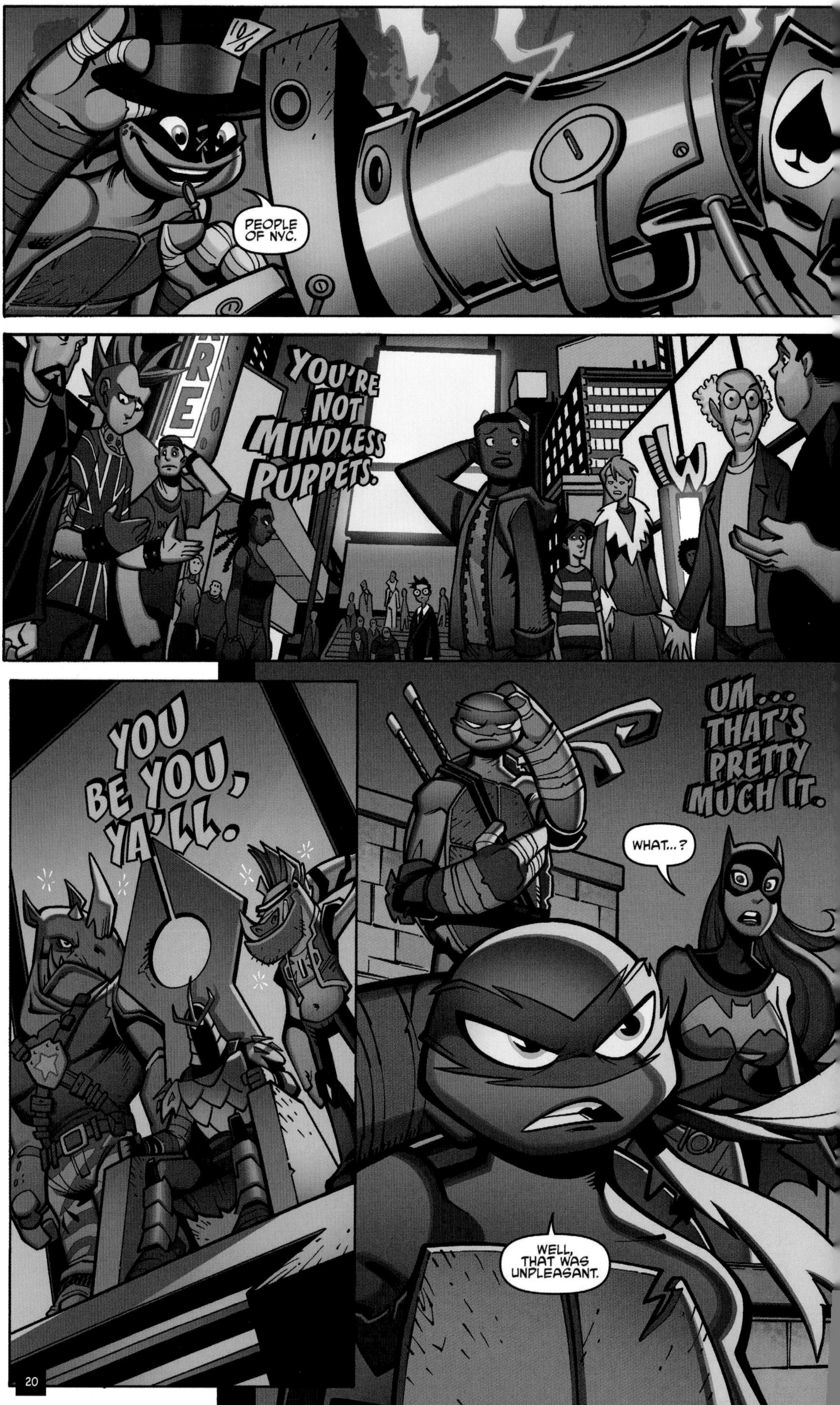

PEOPLE OF NYC.
YOU'RE NOT MINDLESS PUPPETS.
YOU BE YOU, YA'LL.
UM... THAT'S PRETTY MUCH IT.
WHAT...?
WELL, THAT WAS UNPLEASANT.

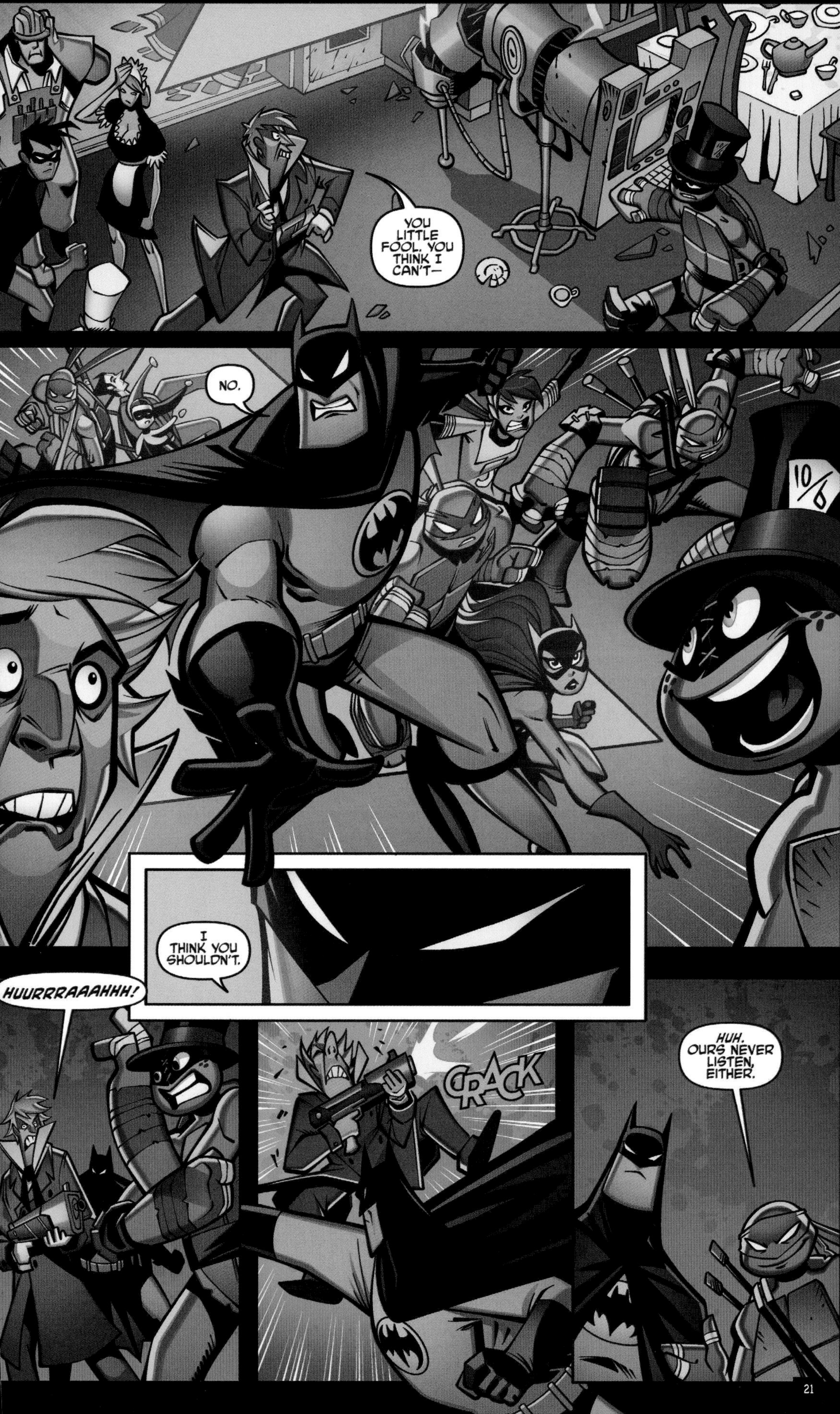
YOU LITTLE FOOL. YOU THINK I CAN'T—
NO.
I THINK YOU SHOULDN'T.
HUURRRAAAHHH!
CRACK
HUH. OURS NEVER LISTEN, EITHER.

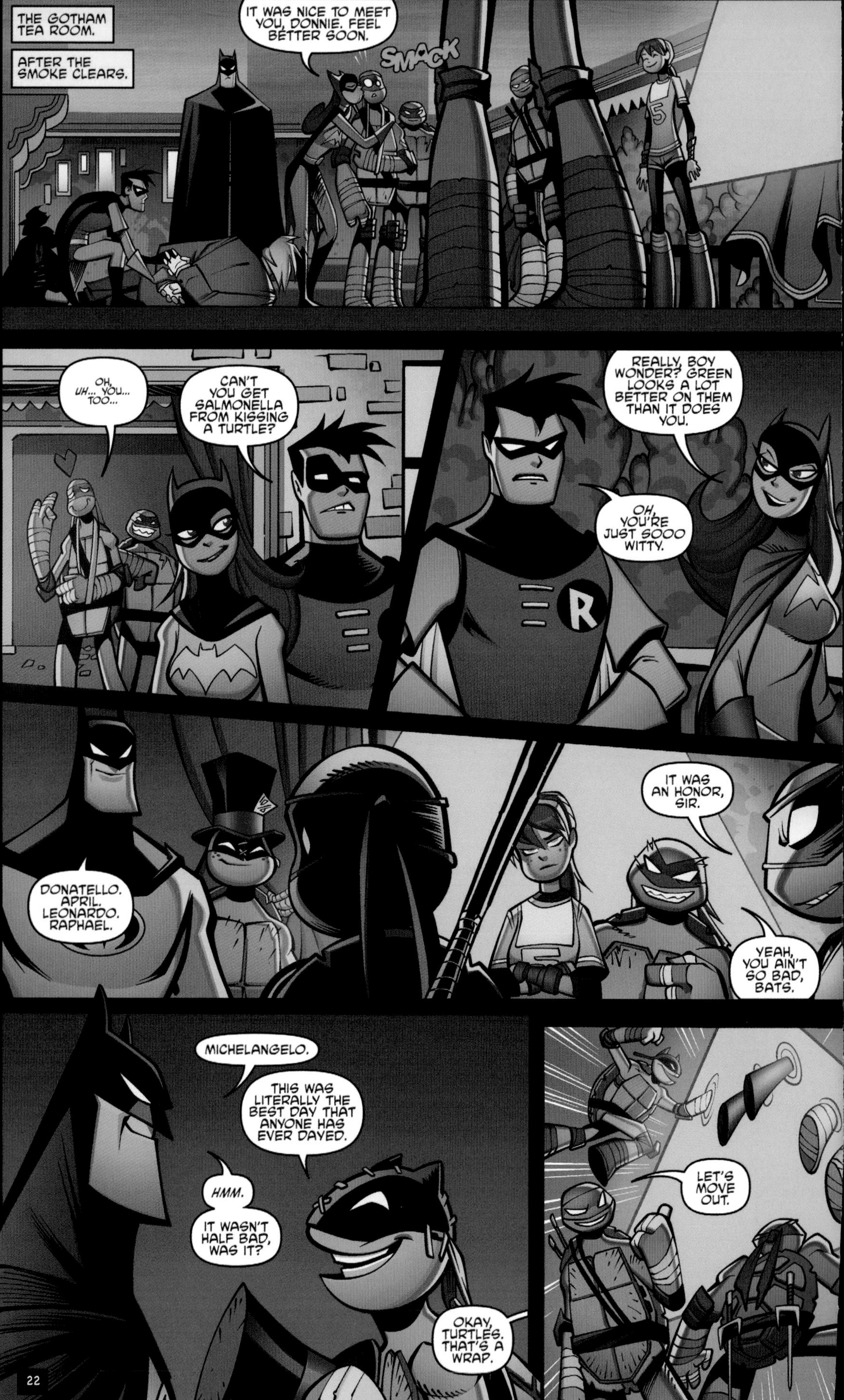
THE GOTHAM TEA ROOM.
AFTER THE SMOKE CLEARS.
IT WAS NICE TO MEET YOU, DONNIE. FEEL BETTER SOON.
SMACK
OH, UH... YOU... TOO...
CAN'T YOU GET SALMONELLA FROM KISSING A TURTLE?
REALLY, BOY WONDER? GREEN LOOKS A LOT BETTER ON THEM THAN IT DOES YOU.
OH, YOU'RE JUST SOOO WITTY.
DONATELLO. APRIL. LEONARDO. RAPHAEL.
IT WAS AN HONOR, SIR.
YEAH, YOU AIN'T SO BAD, BATS.
MICHELANGELO.
THIS WAS LITERALLY THE BEST DAY THAT ANYONE HAS EVER DAYED.
HMM.
IT WASN'T HALF BAD, WAS IT?
OKAY, TURTLES. THAT'S A WRAP.
LET'S MOVE OUT.

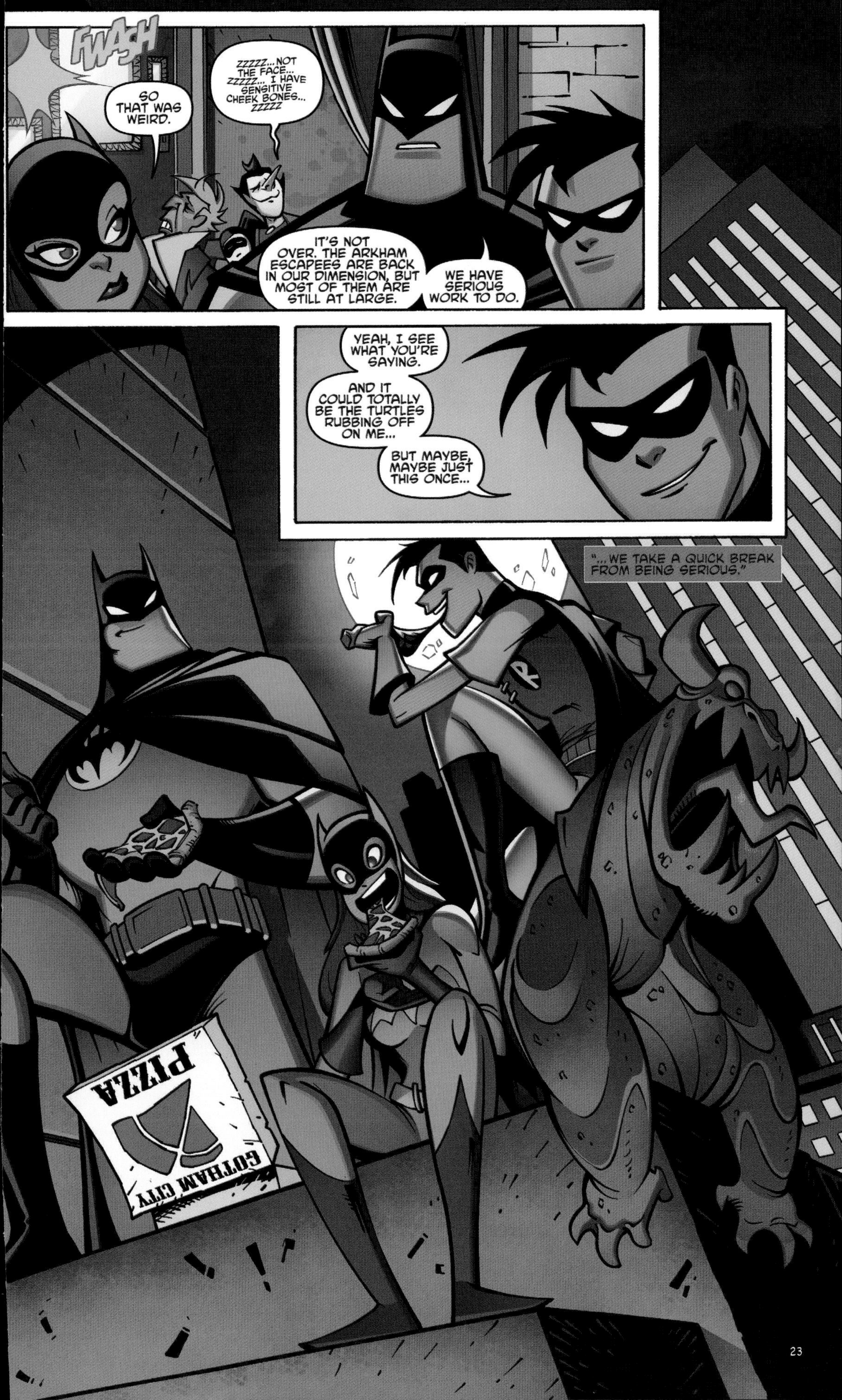
FWASH
SO THAT WAS WEIRD.
ZZZZZ...NOT THE FACE... ZZZZZ... I HAVE SENSITIVE CHEEK BONES... ZZZZZ
IT'S NOT OVER. THE ARKHAM ESCAPEES ARE BACK IN OUR DIMENSION, BUT MOST OF THEM ARE STILL AT LARGE.
WE HAVE SERIOUS WORK TO DO.
YEAH, I SEE WHAT YOU'RE SAYING.
AND IT COULD TOTALLY BE THE TURTLES RUBBING OFF ON ME...
BUT MAYBE, MAYBE JUST THIS ONCE...
"...WE TAKE A QUICK BREAK FROM BEING SERIOUS."
PIZZA
GOTHAM CITY

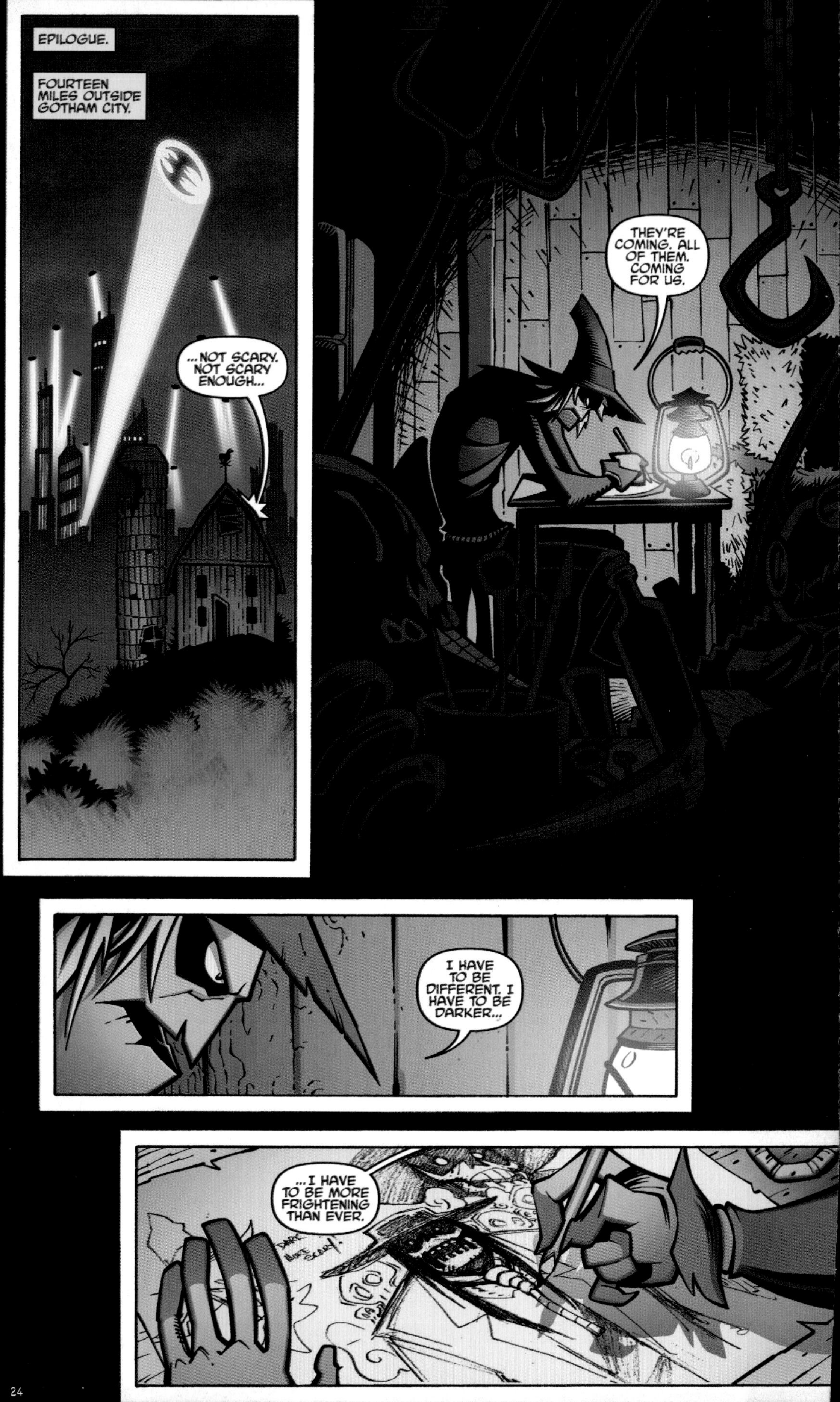
EPILOGUE.
FOURTEEN MILES OUTSIDE GOTHAM CITY.
...NOT SCARY. NOT SCARY ENOUGH...
THEY'RE COMING. ALL OF THEM. COMING FOR US.
I HAVE TO BE DIFFERENT. I HAVE TO BE DARKER...
...I HAVE TO BE MORE FRIGHTENING THAN EVER.
DARK
MORE SCARY!

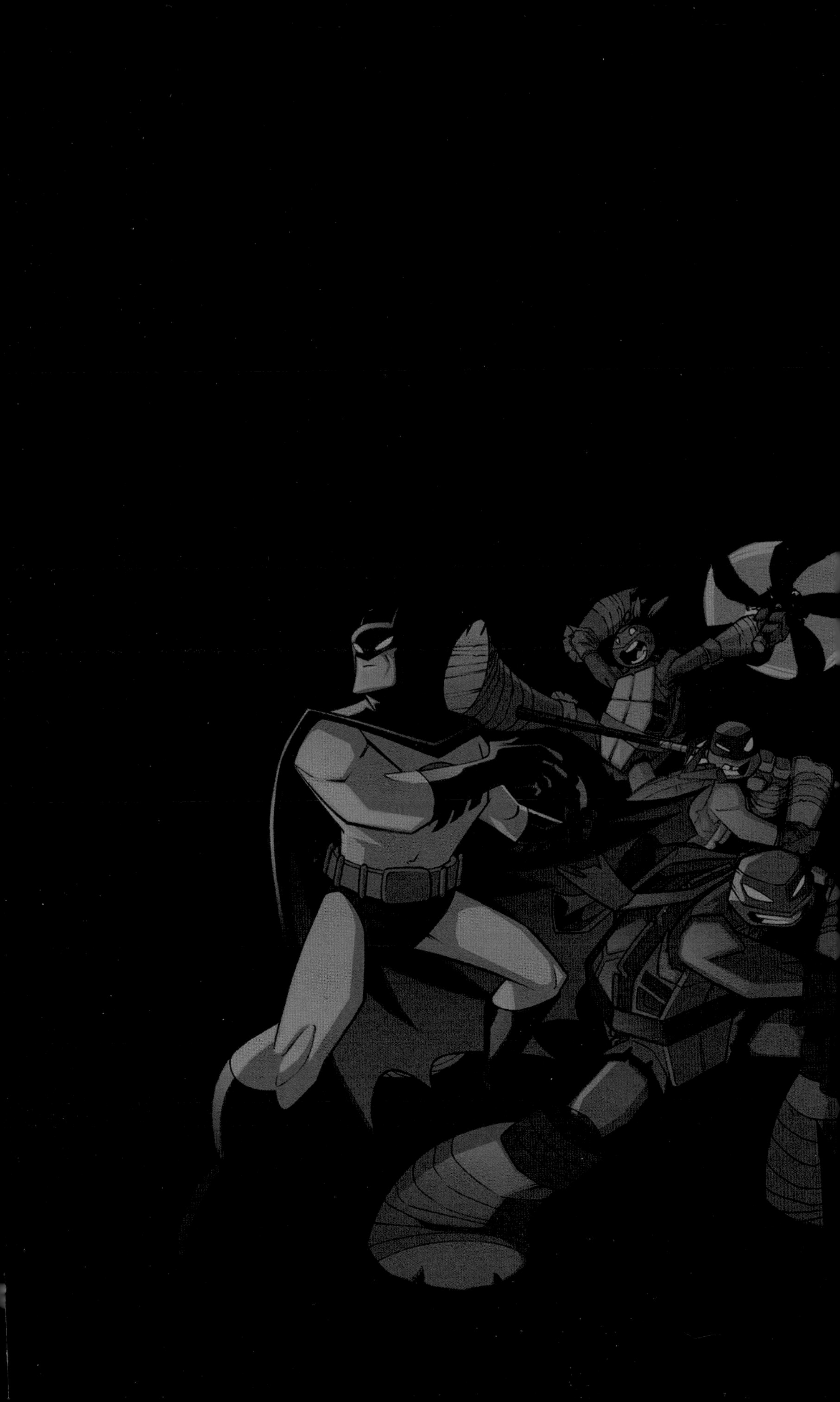

CREATOR

MATTHEW K. MANNING

THE AUTHOR OF THE AMAZON BEST-SELLING HARDCOVER *BATMAN: A VISUAL HISTORY*, MATTHEW K. MANNING HAS CONTRIBUTED TO MANY COMIC BOOKS, INCLUDING *BEWARE THE BATMAN, SPIDER-MAN UNLIMITED, PIRATES OF THE CARIBBEAN: SIX SEA SHANTIES, JUSTICE LEAGUE ADVENTURES, LOONEY TUNES,* AND *SCOOBY-DOO, WHERE ARE YOU?* WHEN NOT WRITING COMICS, MANNING OFTEN AUTHORS BOOKS ABOUT COMICS, AS WELL AS A SERIES OF YOUNG READER BOOKS STARRING SUPERMAN, BATMAN, AND THE FLASH FOR CAPSTONE. HE CURRENTLY RESIDES IN ASHEVILLE, NORTH CAROLINA, WITH HIS WIFE, DOROTHY, AND THEIR TWO DAUGHTERS, LILLIAN AND GWENDOLYN. VISIT HIM ONLINE AT WWW.MATTHEWKMANNING.COM.

JON SOMMARIVA

JON SOMMARIVA WAS BORN IN SYDNEY, AUSTRALIA. HE HAS BEEN DRAWING COMIC BOOKS SINCE 2002. HIS WORK CAN BE SEEN IN *GEMINI, REXODUS, TMNT ADVENTURES,* AND *STAR WARS ADVENTURES,* AMONG OTHER COMICS. WHEN HE IS NOT DRAWING, HE ENJOYS WATCHING MOVIES AND PLAYING WITH HIS SON, FELIX.

GLOSSARY

beacon (BEE-kuhn)—a small radio or signal transmitter, or traditionally a fire or light for a message or warning

canary (kuh-NAIR-ee)—a bright yellow bird known for its singing ability

crusader (kroo-SADE-ur)—a person who tries to change things for the better

dastardly (DAS-turd-lee)—evil or cruel

dynamic (dye-NAM-ik)—skilled, energetic, or powerful

frabjous (FRAB-juss)—a word created by the author Lewis Carroll that means delightful or joyful

frequency (FREE-kwuhn-see)—the speed of vibrations of an electromagnetic wave used for radio communication

gateway (GAYT-way)—a inter-dimensional portal

looking glass (LUK-ing GLASS)—another name for a mirror

manipulate (muh-NIP-yuh-late)—to influence people to do or think the way you want

scurry (SKUR-ee)—to hurry or run with short, quick steps

susceptible (sus-SEP-tee-buhl)—likely to be influenced or harmed

utility (yoo-TIL-uh-tee)—something useful

wonderland (WUHN-dur-land)—a make-believe world created by the author Lewis Carroll

VISUAL QUESTIONS AND WRITING PROMPTS

1. WHY DO YOU THINK THE GUARD BROUGHT MAD HATTER A BOX OF SUPPLIES? HINT: PAY CLOSE ATTENTION TO THE GUARD'S FACE.

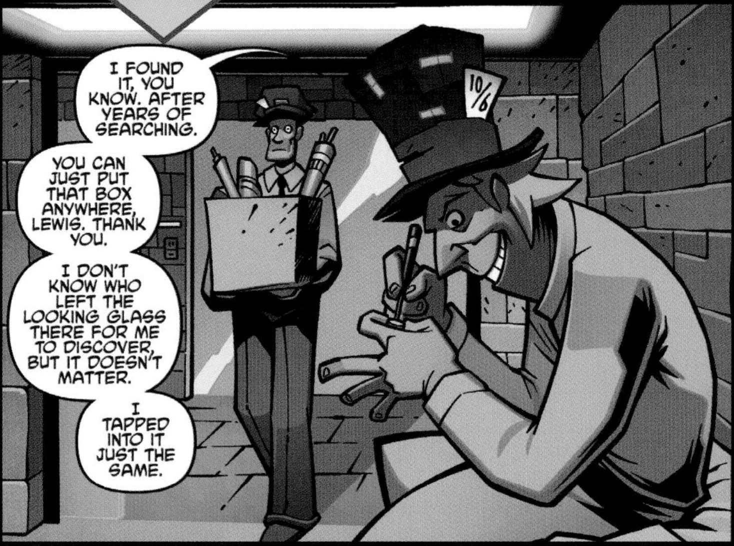
I FOUND IT, YOU KNOW. AFTER YEARS OF SEARCHING.
YOU CAN JUST PUT THAT BOX ANYWHERE, LEWIS. THANK YOU.
I DON'T KNOW WHO LEFT THE LOOKING GLASS THERE FOR ME TO DISCOVER, BUT IT DOESN'T MATTER.
I TAPPED INTO IT JUST THE SAME.
10/6

2. WHY DOES THE GUARD FALL ASLEEP AND HOW DO YOU KNOW THAT MAD HATTER IS BEHIND IT?

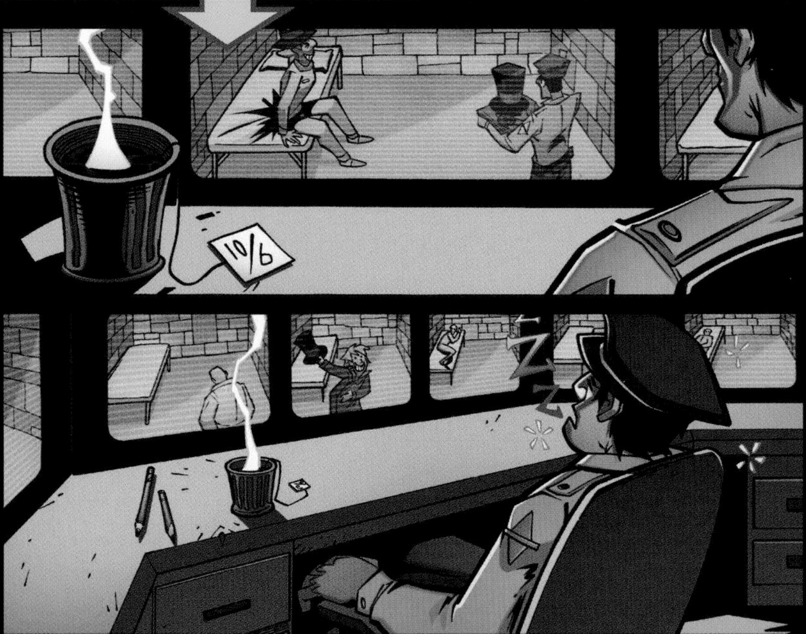
10/6

3. PRETEND THAT MAD HATTER'S PLAN HAD WORKED. WRITE A STORY ABOUT WHAT HAPPENS NEXT.

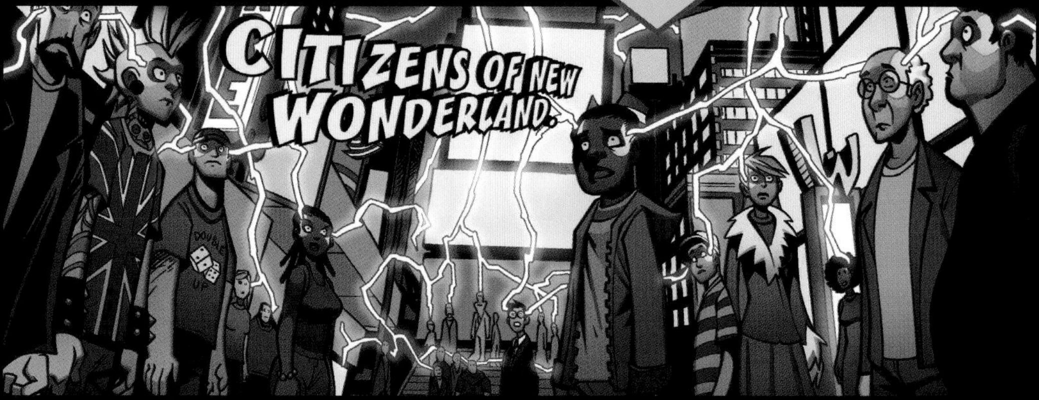
CITIZENS OF NEW WONDERLAND!

4. WHO DO YOU THINK SCARECROW IS TALKING ABOUT IN THE PANEL BELOW?

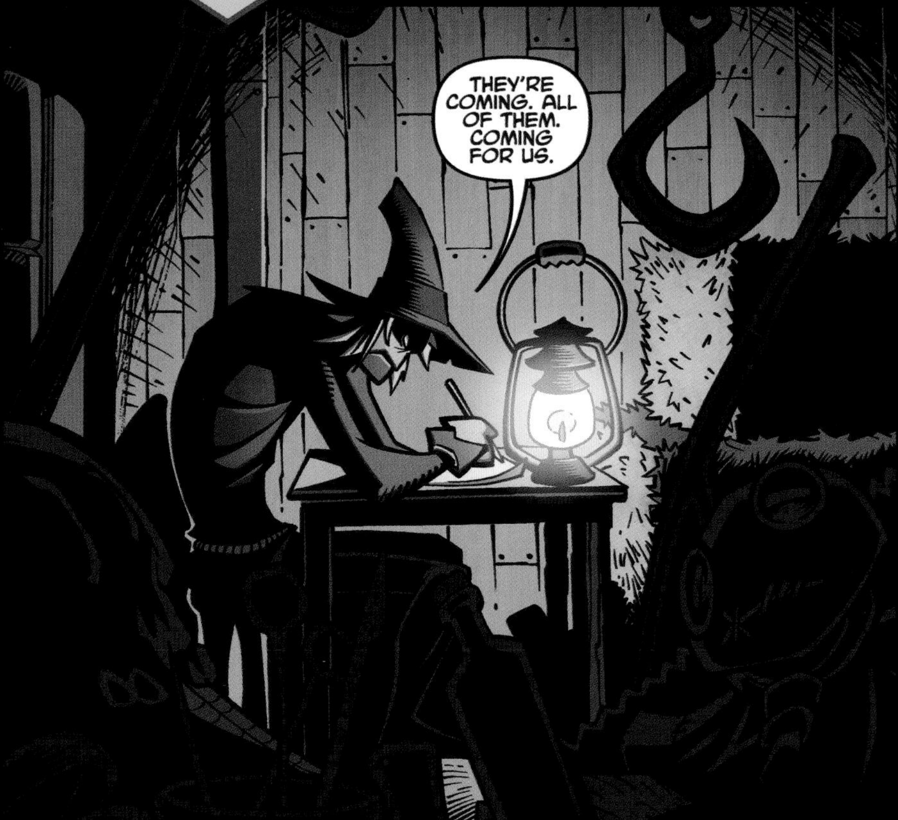
THEY'RE COMING. ALL OF THEM. COMING FOR US.

BATMAN™ TEENAGE MUTANT NINJA TURTLES ADVENTURES

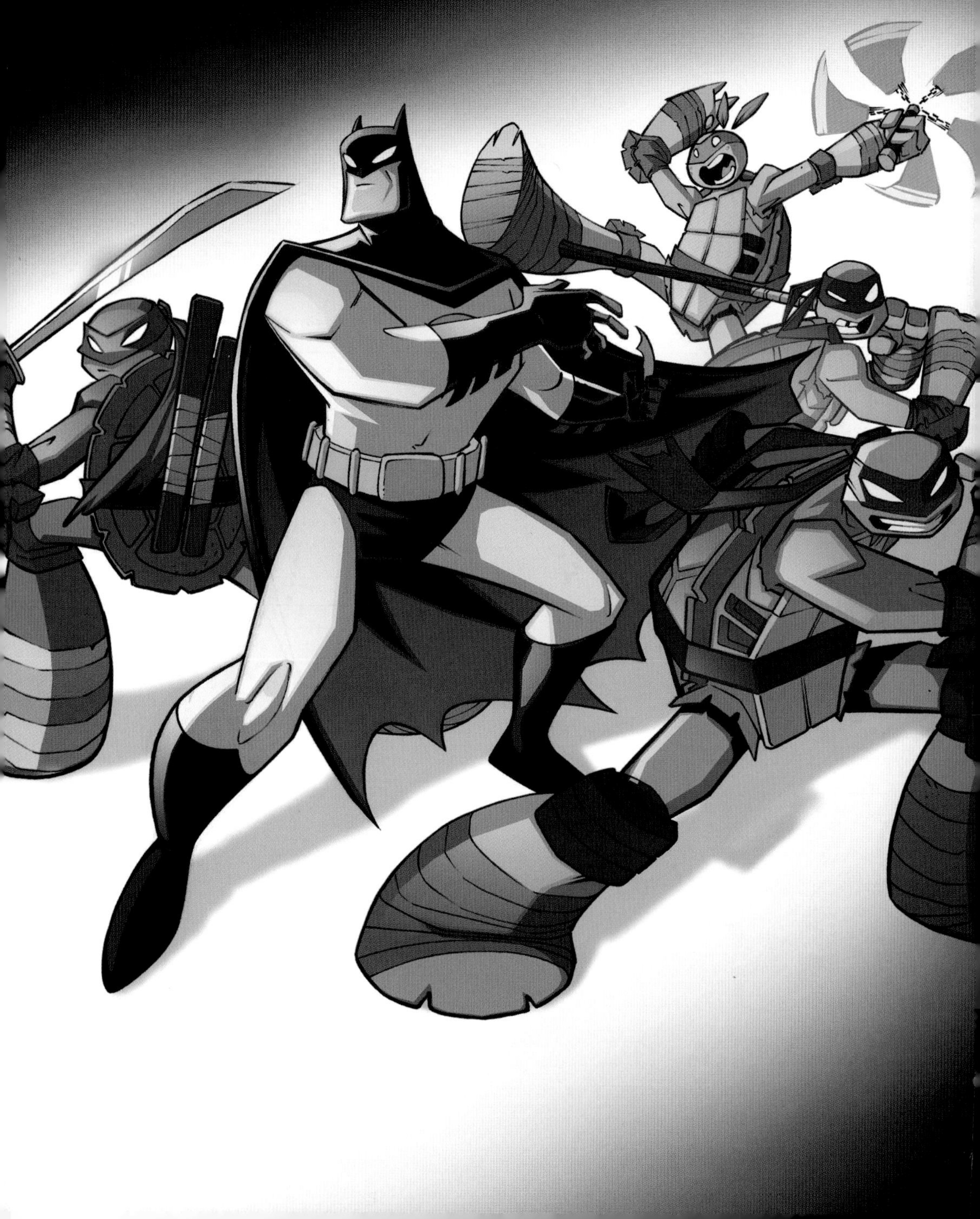

READ THEM ALL!

IDW
BATMAN TEENAGE MUTANT NINJA TURTLES
ADVENTURES
THE FACE OF TWO WORLDS

IDW
BATMAN TEENAGE MUTANT NINJA TURTLES
ADVENTURES
THE CLOWN AND THE CLAN

IDW
BATMAN TEENAGE MUTANT NINJA TURTLES
ADVENTURES
Manning
Sommariva
GREENER ON THE OTHER SIDE

IDW
BATMAN TEENAGE MUTANT NINJA TURTLES
ADVENTURES
TO LAUGH SO NOT TO CRY

IDW
BATMAN TEENAGE MUTANT NINJA TURTLES
ADVENTURES
THROUGH THE LOOKING GLASS

IDW
BATMAN TEENAGE MUTANT NINJA TURTLES
ADVENTURES
Manning
Sommariva
Parsons
Ito
THE TERROR OF THE KRAANG

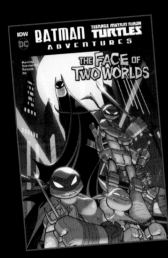

BATMAN™ TEENAGE MUTANT NINJA TURTLES™

ADVENTURES